Eye of the Storm

Eye of the Storm

Lee Rowan

Cheyenne Publishing
Camas, Washington
www.cheyennepublishing.com

ISBN: 978-0-9797773-5-6

Edited by Leslie H. Nicoll

Cover art by Alex Beecroft

Published by Cheyenne Publishing
Camas, Washington
Mailing Address:
     P. O. Box 872412 Vancouver, WA 98687-2412
Website: www.cheyennepublishing.com

Dedication

In Memory of Bill Mitchell: Seer, teacher, and friend. Many thanks to Ann for French geography and Marie for the topsail schooner.

Chapter 1

"Straighten your collar, Commander. And get your hand out of my breeches."

William Marshall, Commander in His Majesty's Royal Navy, choked on a laugh even as he reluctantly disengaged from a passionate, shockingly improper embrace with his dear friend and lover, David Archer. Davy was right, unfortunately. Their carriage was slowing as it reached its destination, and although fifteen minutes had not been near enough, it was more than he'd thought to ever have again.

"My love, I had to come home." Will had been close to tears at that simple statement. He did not deserve such fidelity; he had not expected it. For months he had ignored Davy's letters, a deliberate severance of contact that had been meant to turn his lover away from this unsuitable, dangerous attachment. But it had been to no avail. Davy had refused to accept Will's self-immolation, and rejected the notion that parting was better for either of them. As soon as he had recovered fully from the gunshot wound he'd received on their last mission together, he had set about answering the desire of Will's heart rather than his head, and it was impossible to wish he had done otherwise.

As the doorman at the inn approached to lower the carriage steps, Will glanced once more at Davy, and even the meeting of eyes was like a caress. "Later," Davy said softly. "I did not come all the way from Jamaica for just a carriage ride."

The door flipped open. There was no time to say more.

Their host, who had played coachman to give them a little time along together, dropped from the driver's seat and landed beside them, the capes of his greatcoat settling into neatly-tailored layers about his shoulders. From his sleek brown queue to his polished boots, he was every inch the gentleman spy. "Ready to go to work, Captain?"

"Indeed, Sir Percy," Will said, his heart leaping at being so addressed. He saw that they were at the Spice Island Inn, an establishment generally too rich for his purse. "May I ask whether there are there any more surprises awaiting me?"

"You've had the best, I think, though I expect you'll be pleased to renew Baron Guilford's acquaintance."

Will blinked, then realized that Sir Percy was referring to Davy's cousin, Christopher St. John. "Absolutely, sir," he said as they entered the inn. "What brings his lordship out on such a dirty night?"

"The pleasure of your company, of course."

"How very sad," Will said, feigning worry. "When did his judgment desert him?" He received a cuff from Davy, laughed, and followed Sir Percy inside, to a private dining room where Christopher St. John rose from the head of the table, hand outstretched to greet him. Will shook his hand gladly. He could never repay the kindness Kit had shown him and Davy back in Jamaica, giving them time and freedom to be together that they could never have had under any other circumstances.

"So you've allowed Percy to press you into service,"

Kit said. "Splendid! Come, sit down." He bore a strong resemblance to his cousin, but it was less striking than when they'd first met, years before. A comfortable, settled family life had filled St. John out a bit, while a near-fatal wound and months of convalescence had left Davy thinner and less robust. But both cousins had an irrepressible cheerfulness that made them pleasant company in any circumstance.

"For now, we have bread and butter and good Bordeaux." Kit poured wine into Will's glass and went on, "Supper will be up presently, now that our party is complete. David offered us any odds you'd volunteer."

"I hope you weren't foolish enough to bet against him."

"Of course not. Neither Percy nor I would hazard a penny. What sailor wouldn't seize the chance? I know the sea takes you fellows like strong drink—you must have missed it terribly." His smile said he knew what Will had missed—or rather, whom.

"I did, sir." Will had been given the chair at Kit's left hand, and David took the chair across from him. "But I can hardly complain about my fortunes, with so many of my shipmates set ashore penniless. My half-pay has met my needs, and no man ever died of boredom." *Or loneliness*, he added to himself, meeting Davy's eyes as a foot nudged his beneath the table. "Are you also a part of this new enterprise?"

"Only in a very minor role," Kit said. "I no longer suffer from seasickness as badly as when we first met, but a voyage is no pleasure. I'm home to stay, I hope, though from time to time I shall offer such small assistance as I may."

"It's a great deal more than small assistance," Sir

Percy said, "but there's no need to embarrass him by going into detail. Captain Marshall, how quickly could you find twenty trustworthy men?"

Will was given ample time to consider that question as servants entered the room with dishes whose aroma put even his longing for Davy into perspective. He had not eaten since early afternoon, and while Davy would no doubt stay delightfully warm all night long, that savory meat pie would cool if not dispatched with alacrity. For some minutes conversation was reduced to expressions of appreciation and "please pass the salt."

When Will leaned back in his chair at last, his hunger was sated and his heart overflowing. With a feast before him, Davy restored to him, and a vessel waiting for his hand at the helm, he was in Paradise; he could ask for nothing more.

Well, that was not entirely true. He could wish that Sir Percy would wait until tomorrow to explain his new mission. True Paradise would involve retiring to a bedchamber with his lover and making extensive apologies for abandoning him to what Will had thought he should have—a normal life, a wife and family.

But duty before pleasure was the Navy way, so he forced his attention back to the business at hand, and learned that he was not going to receive orders, as such, when operating in His Majesty's unofficial service. Instead, he was given a general picture of a web of clandestine transport and communication, operated by Sir Percy, which had been spiriting agents in and out of France since before King Louis' execution. His own part in it would be as a courier, ferryman for the occasional English agent, and both sentinel and herald should hostilities break out unexpectedly.

His official title was to be Captain. His ship was the *Mermaid,* a private yacht under the ownership of David St. John, cousin to Baron Guilford who had decided to strike out on his own, speculating, in a small and prudent way, in fine gemstones. Although familiar with the sea, Mr. St. John had decided to hire someone to command the ship, leaving him free to attend to his business.

Davy himself was uncharacteristically quiet during the briefing. Though Will felt the lack of his conversation, he was grateful for the absence of distraction. It was hard enough to keep his eyes off Davy's face and his mind on the job without the constant, inner awareness of that beloved body so near, a feeling like a compass needle seeking true north. By the time the briefing was half over, Will felt his head would burst from all the undigested information stuffed into it. He knew he would not remember all the signs and counter-signs. "There will be a signal-book," he asked hopefully, "or something of the sort?"

"Oh, of course," Sir Percy said. "I'll deliver that myself, just before you sail. We never make a copy until the last possible moment."

"Very good. Thank you." Will found himself growing impatient with the briefing, and annoyed with himself for that impatience. But he knew that the hours were ticking away, and the long autumn night was nearly half-gone. Once he and Davy were aboard ship, they would have to maintain the strictest discretion. That carriage ride had not been nearly long enough.

"One last question," Sir Percy said. "Do you have any business you must attend to before you leave?"

"Nothing that will delay me, sir. I should be able to sail in two days, if the men I have in mind are here in

Portsmouth. I'm certain at least two are here, and they should be able to locate the others. Am I correct in guessing that hiring the right crew is worth a day's delay?"

"Absolutely." The dandified attire Sir Percy affected looked like the costume it was in contrast to that gentleman's focused intelligence. "I meant to give you more time to make arrangements, but you managed to make yourself difficult to locate."

"Had I known you were looking for me, and with such news, I'd have hired the town crier to call your name," Marshall said in all seriousness. "I cannot thank you enough, sir."

"Not at all, Captain. This is not the sort of job that could be handed off to just anyone. I recognize that the schedule presses you hard, but this message must be across the Channel by the end of the week, and that would put you in place for a rendezvous for which you are particularly suited."

"What sort of craft is she?" Marshall asked, as though the answer mattered at all.

"Something you may not have seen before—a topsail schooner. Some shipbuilder's experiment, I think, and a very successful one. She's a sweet little vessel, less than 200 tons—a yacht, really. Four small guns, which I hope you won't need. The *Mermaid's* French-built, a fast courier taken as a prize toward the end of hostilities. Her papers show that she was bought into the service, then sold off when the treaty was signed. She's not much of a fighter, but you shouldn't be going into battle. You may need speed and maneuverability, and she's got those in abundance."

"I'll have her across in time if we have to row ourselves," Marshall promised. "And I can find my men if yours can see to the provisions. The Navy—"

"We shan't be dealing with the Navy's supply line. Just give me a list."

That, of course, meant summoning the innkeeper to bring pen, ink, and foolscap so that Marshall could, with Davy's assistance, compose a list of what he'd need for a cruise of six to eight weeks. Davy couldn't be of much help with the proposed crew roster, since he'd only arrived himself, but there wasn't much they could do about that tonight.

Tomorrow Will would visit Mrs. Quinn, settle his account for his lodging, and see if she could give him the direction of Barrow, who'd helped spirit Davy to safety at Kit's estate in Jamaica. He'd seen some of the men who had served with him hanging about here in Portsmouth, hoping for work. They had all been set ashore when the treaty was signed, and they generally stayed as close as they could to the port, in case a ship might be in need of able seamen. There'd be no problem finding men—even the right men. It would just be a matter of time.

Once the list was written up, Sir Percy perused it. "Much of this is already aboard, I believe, and you'll have the rest by the end of the day tomorrow. Will that do?"

David spoke up at last. "Of course it will. Gentlemen, it's well past one in the morning. If Captain Marshall is to do his job, he must get some sleep. I don't want him wrecking my lovely little yacht because he can't keep his eyes open."

"Your yacht," his cousin scoffed. "You've taken to that role like a duck to water."

"Of course—it's my first honest employment in months." He glanced sidelong at Will, eyes smiling. "Even better, I have at least the facade of command over this elusive rascal."

"I hope you still remember how to work, after months of sloth." Kit said.

If Will had not known how watchful Kit had been of Davy's health and safety while his cousin convalesced at Kit's estate in the West Indies, he'd have thought that an unkind jest. At the time, it had been no laughing matter. "Better you as owner than me," he said. "No one would believe I had the nerve to risk my savings—or savings enough to risk. But Mr. Archer is right, gentlemen. I've so much to keep in mind, I'll be lucky to remember my own name in the morning."

"You're not the one sailing under an alias," David said. "It still seems foolish, now that all that old business is squared away."

"We've taken too many pains to establish David St. John's existence," Sir Percy said. "His ownership of the *Mermaid* is a legal convenience we shall all appreciate if the yacht or her owner finds it necessary to disappear."

"There's nothing easier to hide than a man who never was," Kit agreed. "All joking aside, gentlemen, I am particularly grateful that you are the ones to undertake this mission." He passed round the brandy bottle, and raised his glass. "Here's to the *Mermaid*, her Captain and crew. Success to us, and confusion to Boney!"

They joined the toast with pleasure, and Kit took his leave without further ado. He had hired a house in town where his wife Zoë was waiting—they, too, had been apart for much longer than they would have liked. Sir Percy had other unspecified tasks to attend to, and did not seem surprised when Will declined his offer of a ride back to his lodging house.

⚓ ⚓ ⚓

At last, they were alone together. "Well, Captain Marshall," Davy said cheerfully, "Do you think you would be comfortable sharing my room for what's left of the night?"

"I really must," Will said, feigning regret. "It would be too cruel to rouse Mrs. Quinn from her blameless bed at this late hour."

"I see. Every consideration for Mrs. Quinn—but you don't mind rousing me!" He took a candlestick and lit it from the branch on the table. "Come along, then, you inconsiderate lout. The room's just down this hall."

It was late and their neighbors were no doubt asleep, so Will kept his voice low, teasing. "Do you mean to tell me you would prefer not to be roused?"

"Captain Marshall, if I am not roused at least once before cock-crow I shall be deeply disappointed. Here we are…" He opened the door to a small but very comfortable room, dimly lit by a banked fire. The curtains were closed, and the coverlet turned down in invitation.

Will slid the bolt home on the door and, as always, hung his coat on the doorknob so that it blocked the keyhole. Afloat or ashore, what they were about to do was a hanging offense.

He had barely turned before Davy was in his arms. He was overwhelmed by the warmth of the body pressed against him, the lips opening under his own, the sense of being anchored once more, in a world where he had been set adrift. He suddenly felt whole again, and his body responded to its restoration with a surge of desire.

His hands slid down to Davy's arse. They should have undressed, or at least unbuttoned, but it seemed as though both of them were caught in the desperate need to reaffirm what they had nearly lost. Will leaned back against the wall beside the door as Davy pressed against him, and they stayed like that, moving together, kissing, holding one another, for a time Will could not measure. Was he dreaming? This felt almost unreal, a wish he'd not dared hope to see fulfilled. But his body kept telling him this was no dream. It was real—the reality he had almost thrown away.

Finally Davy pulled back. He looked tipsy. Sounded that way, too. Will felt the same, though they really had not drunk that much wine.

"Let's go to bed, Will."

"Yes." He blew out the candle that Davy had set on the bedside table. They didn't need it anyway; the room was small and the fire's glow was enough. "Wait," he said, as Davy reached for his own waistcoat buttons. "Let me."

Their assignations had most often been brief, stolen moments. There hadn't usually been time for this sort of thing. And they were botching it now, too eager to go slowly. With a head start, Will had his lover unbuttoned first, and slid both coat and waistcoat off, tossing them onto the chair by the window. Things got silly after that, and they wound up leaving shoes scattered and clothes lying in a heap. Will fell back upon the bed and stifled a yelp as the handle of a warming-pan connected with his unprotected rear.

"Mind the reef, sir!" Davy pulled the utensil out and shoved it beneath the bed. Will climbed under the blankets, holding them up so Davy could slip in beside him.

The first touch of skin against naked skin was so beautiful he wanted to weep. How could he have been stupid enough to leave his heart behind? He had not even been alive these past few months. Not until now.

"Sorry..." he mumbled between kisses. "Davy, I'm sorry I was such a fool."

"I'm sorry you were, too," Davy said. "And I have a few choice things to say to you—but not now." He rolled onto Will, pinning him down. "Can you stop thinking for a little while, and simply feel?" The question was accompanied by a long, deep kiss, and a slow undulation of his body all along Will's. By the time his lips were free, Will had forgotten the question. He let his head fall back as Davy's mouth moved down to his throat, brushed against his collarbone. The cool breath on damp skin made him shiver.

Stop thinking...yes. Better to lie back and enjoy his lover's touch, as Davy explored his body with mouth and hands. Weeks of self-denial had almost numbed him, and even though he'd been waiting for this very thing for hours, some small part of his mind kept insisting that this was not wise.

Wise or not, he savored the feeling. There was never time enough for them to be together this way... *Stop thinking.* He gasped aloud as Davy licked one nipple and pinched the other, tangling his fingers in Davy's hair and running his hand down his lover's back. There was muscle there once more, not just skin over ribs. Davy had healed; he was himself again.

Will pulled Davy's head up to taste his mouth, wrapping his legs around Davy's so their bodies were pressed together, their cocks sliding against one another.

"I have some salve," Davy whispered breathlessly.

"Never mind that, this is enough." He caught Davy's arse in both hands, pressing him even closer. It had been so long, he had tried so hard to stop wanting this, that now, when he had his love here in his arms, he was almost afraid to let himself feel.

Warm breath tickled his ear. "What's wrong?"

"Nothing… I cannot believe you're really here."

"Trust me, I'm no incubus." Davy ground against him. "Only flesh and blood—" He shivered. "Oh, *damn,* Will, I can't wait—need you—"

His urgency overwhelmed Will's uncertainty, and their sweat served to smooth the ride; the kissing and touching had brought them both to fever pitch. They rocked together on the sturdy bed, as they had before in other hired rooms, letting the excitement rise and build and finally peak, the sounds of their release muffled in each other's lips.

Davy collapsed atop him. "Oh, my God. I'd forgotten…"

"Yes…" Will held on as Davy tried to roll off, so they wound up lying side by side, arms wrapped around one another. "Why was I such a fool?"

"I don't know. A natural talent, I suppose." Davy yawned. "I think I'm getting old, Will. I may need to sleep before we go again." He chuckled. "Do you remember our first night together, in that coaching inn?"

How could he ever forget? "Did we sleep at all?"

"I don't remember." He couldn't see Davy's smile, but he could hear it in his voice. "Must have. I remember waking, wondering if it was all a dream."

"It still feels like a dream." Will took a deep breath, drawing in the scent of Davy's hair and the lingering aroma of sex. "You said you had things to say—if you mean to tell me I was an idiot, I shan't argue."

"No." Davy was silent for a moment. His hand, roving over Will's chest, came to rest over his heart. "Will, you know I love you; I'll always love you. But I must tell you this: If you ever again leave me like that, go away and stay away, and refuse to answer my letters—I'll not come looking for you a second time."

Whatever Will had expected, it wasn't that, and it frightened him. "I—I didn't think you would. Not this time, or ever."

"I had to, Will. I had to know why. It nearly sent me mad, wondering. I was almost ready to do myself in—"

Will's arms tightened convulsively. "I didn't realize—"

"I could not understand why you refused to answer me." There was pain in Davy's voice, and a ghost of frustration. "But once you sent that damnable sonnet, I guessed you were only being noble and stupid. You and I have nothing to do with Shakespeare and his dark lady— or his dark laddie, either."

Will shook his head. "Not noble. Stupid, perhaps. I only wanted you to have a better life."

"There is no better life," Davy said with certainty. "Not for me. But if you'd decided to try for a proper officer's life—a wife and children—Will, for all I knew you might have met a girl. If not for me, you'd have found yourself a wife by now—a sweetheart, at least. You should, you know—once you make Post Captain, it will look peculiar if you don't settle down."

"Oh, for heaven's sake! I've never wanted anyone else."

"You never had a chance to look for anyone else," Davy said sagely. "You're the one who should be thinking of a better life. I have no military ambition, but you'll make Post before long."

It might have been the late hour, or the wine, but Marshall found himself completely muddled. "Do you truly want me to do that?"

"It's nothing to do with what I want. I should love to find a place we could just live quietly together. What I want is simply not possible. But, Will, marriage is what's expected if you mean to stay in the Navy, and I know you do. Since you don't have rank or position outside the service, your ambition would be best served by finding a wife who can advance your social standing."

"And where would that leave you?"

Davy was quiet for a moment that spun out in the darkness. "That depends on you, I suppose, and on what sort of marriage you might make. For some women, it seems to be more or less a business transaction, trading an heir for security, with hardly any feeling involved. And so many married men have mistresses... I suppose we would contrive." He yawned hugely. "I'm sorry if I sound cynical, Will, but one of my own sisters married her husband in order to have her own establishment. She was quite pragmatic about it. She's given him a son and she's a splendid hostess, but according to my other sister they seldom even sleep in the same house. If you had that sort of businesslike arrangement, you would be safer."

"I don't—"

"We'd both be safer," Davy insisted. "And if we were at sea, your wife would be her own mistress most of the time—or even someone else's. I wouldn't mind sharing, if she didn't."

Marshall was a bit shocked at Davy taking this line, though to be honest, a nice, safe, affectionate marriage—certainly not a business arrangement—was exactly what Will had been thinking would be best for his lover. But even though what Davy suggested was true, Will didn't want to find some unsuspecting woman and marry her for public appearance. It would be the most despicable sort of lie, and he already felt like ten kinds of a scrub. "I don't deserve you."

"Very likely not, but you've got me." Davy took the harshness out of the words with a kiss. "We'd better sleep now, if we can. We'll have no rest tomorrow—or later this morning, to be precise."

"That's true. As early as possible, I must locate Barrow. He's a proper bosun, he'll know where to find the men we need. Old Calypsos, if we can find them."

"And I must take a letter to your landlord, pay your shot, and pack your dunnage. You'll be busy enough here. There'll be no time left for such errands once you start hiring."

"Oh, Lord, I'd forgotten him. Yes, if you would. Thank you."

"A command enters your mind and all else flies out." Davy's lips brushed across Will's. "I'll be playing second fiddle to a mermaid."

"You'll play second fiddle to no one," Will said. "Besides, I can't take a ship to bed."

"Lucky for me." Davy said, stretching luxuriously. "But it's too bad we can't take this bed to the ship. Come morning it's back to separate hammocks and best behavior."

At this moment, warm and sleepy and sated, Will felt as though he had all he would ever require. "Oh, I'm sure we'll find time now and then."

"Until we sail you won't have a moment to spare." Davy flung an arm across Will's body and nestled against his shoulder. "But at least we're together now. Goodnight, Will."

Chapter 2

Sometime later, Marshall woke in the darkness to find himself wrapped around a familiar form, and fought to stay asleep so the dream would not vanish. Then Davy wriggled his rump backwards and rolled over for a kiss, and Will remembered this was real.

"Are you asleep?" Davy murmured.

"Yes. And I'm having a wonderful dream."

A soft laugh. "You fool." Davy touched his face, his thumb trailing across Will's lips as the hand brushed down the side of his neck and shoulder. "Do you have any idea how I've missed you?"

"Oh, possibly." He ruffled a hand through Davy's hair, thinking of the beautiful golden mane that had been sacrificed to disguise earlier that year. "I'm glad you gave me your pigtail, but this suits you."

"You'll need your own mop tidied. Only the oldest sea-dogs are still wearing the queue." Davy pulled him close for another kiss, forestalling a reply. The taste of him drove away thought, and Will realized he wasn't going to get much sleep this night.

He couldn't find it in him to care. The feel of Davy's hands upon him, the sharp intake of breath when he licked the side of his lover's neck, then blew upon it, laughing softly as Davy shivered. "Do you want that salve now?"

"Yes, wait…" He let go enough for Davy to be able to

reach down into the bag that held his things, and prepare himself. This was worth taking time for; Davy was right, they would not have time later. He reached between them to find Davy once again roused and ready, as he was himself.

"Lie back," he suggested. The last time they'd been together, Davy had been too recently wounded to risk Marshall lying atop him, though he liked that best of all. Was he healed enough for that now? Will hovered over him, kissing down his chest, capturing a nipple as he pinned Davy's legs together, running his fingers down one side of his body, then the other, steering him like the finest ship that ever sailed. Their cocks rubbed against one another, delicious friction that made him want more, and he moved up for another kiss, their voices the barest whispers in the dark.

"Will—Oh, *yes!*"

"Is it safe now? For you, I mean."

"It should be. Do you want to?"

"Are you mad? Wanted nothing else since I first saw you." He shifted his weight so Davy could open his legs, then raised his lover's hips and slid sweetly home, feeling like a ship come home to harbor at last.

Davy groaned and he froze. "Does that hurt—*ow!*" A sharp pinch to his arse made him thrust forward, and Davy pushed back against him, turning the movement into a gentle rocking as he wrapped his legs around Marshall's so he could not get away.

"It feels *good*, Will. For pity's sake, don't stop!"

It was worth taking the time to make love properly, and as they moved together, Will lost track of everything but the sensations, spreading from his belly and balls until it burst like fire throughout his whole body. Davy gasped a moment later, thrusting against him and then falling back with a satisfied sigh. "To answer your question," he whispered, "Yes. I'm fine. Never felt better. And the towel is under your pillow."

Marshall dipped his head to catch Davy's half-open mouth and kissed him into silence, savoring the sweetness he'd missed so much. "Confident, weren't you?" he asked.

"Well, since you ask—yes. Here, give me the towel."

Davy wiped the stickiness off them both; they would wash the cloth out tomorrow, when they shaved, another little precaution that was a constant reminder of the vigilance they must maintain.

It was worth the effort, worth the lost sleep. However tired he'd be in the morning, Will didn't grudge a moment. But he fell asleep immediately, a sleep deeper than any he'd known since the last time they'd lain together.

⚓ ⚓ ⚓

A loud, staccato noise hauled him up like an anchor from the deep. It resolved into a thumping on the door, and Marshall blinked as he tried to remember where he was. This late in the year, the sun took its time rising; it was still dark outside.

Davy was already up, struggling into his nightshirt. He opened the door, admitting a servant boy who carried in the shaving water that had been requested the night before. After the boy left Will sat up, then swung his legs over the side of the bed. The bare floorboards were cold against his equally bare feet, but the sensation helped him wake up. He needed a moment to soothe his rattled nerves before he felt prepared to apply the edge of a razor to his face.

"I've ordered hot chocolate brought up," Davy said,

closing the door, "and rolls with butter. We can put those in our pockets if you mean to run off immediately."

"I do mean to run, but not this instant." Will caught his hand and pulled him down for a quick kiss. "My God, I've missed you. Not only this—" he stroked Davy's naked thigh, "but just having you here to talk to."

Davy leaned closer, bending down to kiss the top of Will's head. "Yes. But there's no time for either now, is there?" He smiled ruefully and turned to his own shaving gear. "I do wish we could find ourselves a little cottage somewhere, at least until the war resumes. But you'll be happier with a deck underfoot, and perhaps I will be, too."

Perhaps? Not wanting to borrow trouble, Will said nothing, focusing instead on scraping the stubble off his face. He hoped that Davy was truly well enough to undertake this mission, and that he really wished to do so. How ridiculous if would be if each of them had signed on because he thought the other wanted him to.

But no… That was not true in his own case. Even if there'd been no David Archer thrown into the bargain, wild horses could not have kept William Marshall away from the deck of that schooner. He'd never realized how fully his own existence had centered around life aboard ship, where one's whole world was comprised of a few dozen, or at most a few hundred faces. The clutter of buildings in Portsmouth, the ever-changing panoply of people and carts and beasts, the sheer noise of a busy port—it was one thing to spend a few days ashore now and then, a pleasant diversion. To be trapped here in the crush of humanity, with the crowds and stink and the swooping gulls screaming his own longing to be out and away, running before the wind with all canvas set…

"Ahoy, Captain Marshall!"

He jumped, and nearly cut himself. *"What?"*

"Breakfast is served." Davy slid the tray onto the table beside the shaving pan. "Out at sea, weren't you?" he asked shrewdly. "'Spill your wind and eat your wittles,' as *Calypso's* old cook used to say."

"Sorry," Will said with a smile. "You're right, I was wandering. It seems an age since I've been at sea. I do miss it, Davy. I'd begun to wish I'd never made Commander. There are so few vessels in that class, and every one spoken for."

"You'll be glad of the rank when war resumes. Even if you hadn't been promoted, there seem to be a dozen lieutenants for every post in what remains of the fleet."

Will nodded, breathing in the delicious aroma of hot chocolate. "Two dozen, at least. Perhaps more. And now this, after I'd given up all hope—how can I thank you?"

"Don't be foolish." Davy split open a roll, steam rising in the cool morning air. "I hardly slept since we made landfall, for worrying that you might have found someone else."

"I hope you've done with that, at least!" Will sipped the chocolate, spread butter on one of the fragrant rolls. "In order to find something, one must seek it, I think—and I have no talent for such things even had I the interest, which I do not. I must be like one of those birds that mates for life—I feel jealous when a shopgirl so much as smiles at you."

Davy looked up quickly. "No, really?"

"Yes—so, if you please, no advances toward the vicar's wife when you return his cart and collect my seachest."

With a grin, Davy asked, "Is she pretty?"

"She's a handsome woman," Will began. Davy's eyebrows shot up, and he could not resist laughing. "She's also about twice our age, and properly disdainful of young gallants, as she told me when I made my manners. But they've both been kind to me; I shall miss them." He finished off the last of his breakfast. "And I'll miss the chance to find Barrow if I don't shake a leg. Come, I'll take you to the stable where I left the vicar's cart."

"One moment." Davy leaned against the door and pulled Will into a kiss. Will didn't object, and he didn't hurry; this last touch of lips and body would have to last them both till God knew when. But he didn't dawdle, either. He could hear his *Mermaid* calling.

"Stop here, Davy."

Archer checked the mare, a docile, obedient creature whose thick winter coat let her disregard the drizzly November rain. "Where's the house?"

Will nodded toward the short road to his left. "Just three doors down. I'll get out here. You can continue along this street, then take the first left turn at the apothecary on the corner. I'll meet you down at the Sally Port, then, sometime before noon?"

"Oh, I'll find a boat to bring me out. I remember where we moored her, you know."

David Archer exchanged a discreet hand-clasp with his lover, then watched until Will reached the door of the rooming-house. He looked back with a quick, bright smile, and disappeared inside. With a sigh, Archer lifted the reins and started the vicar's horse back toward her home. He was nearly there before he realized that in the excitement of their reunion, neither he nor Will had really considered the details of this expedition. Once he returned the cart, he would have no way to haul Will's dunnage back to the *Mermaid.* He would have to throw himself on the mercy of Mrs. Merriman, the vicar's wife, and trust her to find a solution.

The rain had let up by the time he found the place, the house abandoned but for a girl in the kitchen. Ten or twelve years of age, she was cleaning dishes and minding a bowl of rising bread dough.

"Missus is gone out," she said.

"Yes, I had gathered that. Will she be back soon?"

"Maybe."

Her small face set in a resolute frown, she said nothing more until she'd finished punching down the dough and replacing the damp cloth that covered it. "Legget's baby is sick, she took 'em some broth. Likely she'll stay awhile."

"Do you know where Mr. Marshall's cottage is?"

"Cowpath out back, past t' pond."

"Thank you very much for your trouble." He placed a penny on the table and left her staring at it, round-eyed, hurriedly wiping her hands on her apron.

He led the horse down the cowpath, hoping the wheels would not lodge in the rutted, squelching mud. The cottage was a simple thing, one front room with a sleeping room beyond it, and the usual out back. The door had no lock, only the simplest latch. It had probably been the original parson's cottage, thriftily kept in repair down through the years.

The bedroom was like a monk's cell. Will's uniforms, one dress, one second-best, and one everyday wear, were folded in his sea chest, along with stockings and winter drawers. Beneath these were his navigational instruments and reference books, and a few odds and ends. Four shirts and two pair of trousers—one threadbare, the other Sun-day-best—were folded neatly on a low shelf beside the bed, with a well-worn deck of playing cards tucked beneath the shirts, no doubt to spare the religious sensibilities of his landlord.

Archer made a mental note to see whether he could find a tailor in town who'd be able to produce a respectable merchant-captain's coat using Will's uniforms as a guideline. A proper merchant did not want a seedy-looking captain at the wheel…and Will did look splendid when he was properly dressed.

Three books lay on the small table by the window of the clean but Spartan room, holding down the latest copy of the *Naval Gazette*. The first was a Bible, which, according to an inscription on the flyleaf, belonged to the household, the second a well-thumbed book of navigational mathematics—how Will could find such material soothing to read, Archer did not understand—and the last was a pocket diary.

He meant to restrain his curiosity, but he could not resist a peek—just one quick look, he would close the book immediately if there was anything inside he should not see… But there was not. The book was nothing more than a record of Will's efforts to find a ship, or even a shore assignment, dating from the moment he'd arrived in Portsmouth until just a week ago. There were a few captains' names at the end, two with "London?" behind them, one without a location. Nothing more.

What had Will been doing all that time? From March to November, this dreary, fruitless search, all to no avail. The cards… Yes, he could imagine Will laying them out in endless games of patience, creating order in the random fall of numbers. He might have borrowed books, too, and newspapers, but what a bleak life this must have been!

Well, that was ended now. Life would be back to normal.

At least it would be for Will. If Commander Marshall felt back on an even keel, Archer himself was now adrift. And he had been drifting ever since he began to recover, back at Kit's plantation in Jamaica.

He still loved the sea, the fresh, open expanse of sun and water and the sense of purpose that came with travel. The voyage home had been a delight, even when they ran into dirty weather. It had been good to be active again, back in motion, sailing somewhere with something important to do.

But to sail only as a means to bringing other men to their end? That no longer held the attraction it once had. After a few months of watching his cousin's painstaking efforts to reform an operation based on the slavery Kit despised into something he could take pride in, Archer found his own priorities changing. He knew that so long as Bonaparte was trying to take over the world, he was honor-bound to oppose that empire, but he had come to the point where glory seemed pretty hollow in comparison to the devastation wrought in winning it.

It wasn't fear; at least, he did not think it was fear, even though he sometimes woke with the memory of smoke erupting from a pistol, and a blow to his side, and darkness. It wasn't that. Having come so near to death, it was somehow easier to accept its inevitability. But where was the meaning in a life dedicated to bringing death? Surely there were better things a man could do with the time he was given.

Nothing could be that simple, of course. If it had only been a matter of philosophy, he could have walked away from the Navy without a second thought. But if there was one constant left in Archer's life, it was Will Marshall. He could imagine life without war; he could imagine life without the Navy—he had, after all, only joined to avoid being sent to serve in his brother's Army regiment. But life without Will—no. It was unthinkable. And Will still wanted him, so for the moment he had both purpose and direction, and would let fate carry him where it would.

Hands on his hips, Archer made one last survey of the austere room. He lifted up the pillow, in case there might be a book or anything beneath, but there was nothing. And there should be. He wasn't sure what he was looking for, but he knew he was missing something. They'd be far away soon, and no way to nip back and retrieve— Oh, of course.

He knelt and peered beneath the bed, grinning when he saw a pair of worn felt slippers and a small wooden box that he recognized from their days at sea. The keepsake box—Will kept his watch in it, and a ring that had been his mother's, and a few other personal things.

This was what he'd been looking for—he knew Will would not have abandoned it. Archer looked inside, just to make sure everything was there. It wasn't prying, Will had shown him the box's contents ages ago. And there, lying atop the varied souvenirs of a sailor's life, were the handful of letters Archer had sent him over the past few months, neatly folded, their sealing wax...intact.

Unopened.

He'd never even read them.

Archer swallowed, then closed the box quickly and placed it, along with the slippers, into Will's sea chest. He wrestled the thing outside and into the cart, led the mare to the house, and found the stout, pink-cheeked Mrs. Merriman back in command of her kitchen. Archer delivered Will's letter, paid his week's rent and added his own thanks for her care of his friend.

"Oh, 'twas nothing," she said. "Poor lad, with no family nor friends to go home to. You tell him he's welcome here any time, and we'll remember you both when we pray for the ships at sea."

"Thank you, ma'am. Now, if I might impose upon you further," he smiled apologetically, "I realized on my way here that I could not return your horse and cart and also return Mr. Marshall's sea chest to him in Portsmouth. Might there be anyone in the household who could drive to town with me, and bring the rig back?"

She frowned thoughtfully. "If you've tuppence to spare, I'm sure Roger, at the livery stable, would jump at the chance. His sister Rachel helps me here, days, and like as not their mother will send him to fetch her home. I believe he'd be happier to come in the cart than afoot."

That settled, Archer left a few shillings for the poor-box, knowing there was always need in the families of sailors set ashore without a penny. Glad to be on the last leg of the journey, he turned the patient mare toward town once more.

He had time to think on the drive back, and decided at last to just leave well enough alone for now. There were all sorts of reasons why Will might have left his letters unopened. It wasn't something Archer could have done; curiosity would have driven him to open the first, and once he'd read the letter nothing could have kept him from writing back. That was probably just as true for Will. And Will had obviously decided not to communicate, no matter what it cost, so of course the easiest way would be to not even look.

He might bloody well have asked me first!

Archer sighed, giving himself a mental thump. There was no point fretting over the past. Will's reaction to his return had told him everything he really needed to know. Will had been a fool, yes—and he'd admitted that readily. It would be cruel to hound him further.

But after all those months of loneliness, it was hard not to feel hurt—and just a little angry.

Archer's mood lifted when he drew close enough to town that he could smell the sea. This had been his choice, every bit as much as Will's; he had engineered it, after all. They would be together again, just as they'd always wanted, at least for the present. The future... Well, the future would have to sort itself out, and that was beyond his control in any case.

The lad at the livery stable turned out to be none other than Roger, who promptly accepted the errand to Merriman's with alacrity and was more than willing to haul Will's sea chest to the Sally Port while Archer ran his errand to the tailor. That last chore was easier than he expected—a few officers had sold their spare uniforms for ready cash, and the tailor found one of fine wool broadcloth that could easily be altered to a landsman's coat by the end of the day. He could tell Will it was a late birthday present, or that he'd bought the new clothing for the pleasure of admiring him in it—and helping him out of it. That was certainly true, in any case.

Archer took delight in giving Will presents, and he was smiling when he left the tailor's and walked down to the Sally Port. It was too easy, in these hard times, to find a boatman willing to row him out to where the elegant *Mermaid* floated at anchor. He picked the thinnest-looking man, in a weathered boat whose larboard oar was handled by a scrawny boy who barely looked big enough to man it. He turned his collar up against the biting wind off the water, and settled himself on the hard wooden seat.

"Shoreboat ahoy!" someone called out as they drew near. He recognized that voice—their old bosun, Barrow, one of the few among the *Valiant's* crew who knew that Lieutenant Archer had survived the gunshot he'd suffered aboard during that final skirmish. Will had found him, then. That was one thing less to worry about, and Archer found himself smiling at Barrow's incorrect greeting. Strictly speaking, that phrase was only used to greet a boat bearing an officer, and the *Mermaid* was a civilian vessel.

Still, it was good to see an old shipmate, and he could not resist returning Barrow's salute once he'd scrambled up the side and onto a deck swarming with busy sailors. "It's only *Mr.* St. John, Barrow," he said under his breath.

"Aye, sir, but it's good to see you lookin' so well." The older man, who'd known both him and Will since they were midshipmen, smiled with an almost fatherly affection. "Back from the dead, and there's few I've seen so sorely missed."

Archer wasn't easily embarrassed, but he was now. "Yes, well..." Glancing around the deck, he said, "I see Klingler, Jules Owen—is Joey Owen aboard too?" He was not surprised to see Barrow nod; the Owen boys were twins and alike as two peas. "Spencer as well..." But not Will, oddly enough. "Are there any other old Calypsos aboard?"

"Bentley and Korthals, sir. They're still ashore, seein' if they can fetch a few more good 'uns. Our boys all know your name, never fear. We won't forget—we're that glad of a berth, we'd call you Queen o' the May if you wanted. Captain Marshall's below, sir."

"I'll look for him there, then. So, what do you think of our *Mermaid*? Will she do?"

"Oh, aye." Barrow squinted up at the rigging, all sails neatly furled. "She's a bit fancy for the likes of us—sails white as a French whore's bottom—but she'll do till we get back on a proper man o' war."

That was high praise, for to Barrow no vessel could ever live up to their old frigate, *Calypso*. Archer nodded and went below. The stern cabin was empty, but he could hear Will's voice echoing from the starboard bow. It sounded as though he was instructing some crewmen on how best to arrange ballast—no one else ever did that job to Will's complete satisfaction, and his rebalancing cargo always seemed to eke out just a bit more speed. There'd be no point going forward to greet him and stumbling into the middle of that chore. This sleek, narrow hull had no room to spare for spectators while boxes and barrels were being slung about.

Archer debated whether to go back on deck, but decided it would be best to let the crew settle in under Barrow's watchful eye. He went on into the cabin and made himself comfortable on the bench seat built under the stern window. As titular owner, the best berth on the ship was his by right, but this was properly the Captain's cabin and it was only logical that he'd be sharing it with the man commanding the vessel. He'd stored some of his own possessions in the cupboards beneath the bench, but left half of them empty for Will's belongings—a superstitious act, perhaps.

He didn't know what Will's plans were for the rest of the day—hunting for crew, most probably. But in the meantime, what was there for him to do? He wondered, again, if he had made a mistake in arranging this. Yes, he would be with Will—that was important, of course it was. But in what capacity? He had no real role on this vessel. He had a packet of gemstones, and the names of some men to contact in France, but for the moment he had no tasks to complete nor any idea of what Will would want him to do.

Still, he was the ship's owner, was he not? He could stroll about on deck if he chose. Or he could stay below out of the weather, and let Captain Marshall establish himself as the one in command.

That seemed the better course of action, all in all. Archer hung his greatcoat on a convenient hook and fished in the pocket for the book he'd been reading the day before, a suitable tale for a man taking ship with no notion of what the future would bring. And a bit of wishful thinking, too—he'd rather be on an Uninhabited Island with Will at this moment than on the finest ship ever built.

Archer smiled, glancing at the title: *The Life and Strange Surprizing Adventures of Robinson Crusoe, of York, Mariner: Who lived Eight and Twenty Years, all alone in an uninhabited Island on the Coast of America, near the Mouth of the Great River of Oroonoque; Having been cast on Shore by Shipwreck, wherein all the Men perished but himself. With An Account how he was at last as strangely deliver'd by Pyrates. Written by Himself.* He suspected Mr. Defoe had missed Shakespeare's injunction naming brevity the soul of wit.

Chapter 3

"Sea-furl the squaresail," Marshall said, squinting into the mix of fog and snow that surrounded the *Mermaid* and cloaked the distant shore of Normandy in a bone-chilling mist. "We can make it pretty when the weather lets up."

"Aye, sir." Barrow took a step away on the tiny quarterdeck and shouted Marshall's instructions up to the topmen clinging to slippery footropes as they wrestled the wet, icy sails onto the single yard. They could expect filthy weather at this time of year, but it hardly seemed fair for it to come on so suddenly.

The day before had been bright and unseasonably warm for early December. Their unscheduled meeting with a merchant vessel bound for England with her hold full of wine had given Davy the chance to trade a ham for a few bottles of unusually palatable burgundy. Getting into his role, Davy had even inquired whether the ship's captain had any interest in a great bargain on nicely-cut amethysts. Although he expressed polite admiration of the stones, the Frenchman had shown no interest in buying any. He'd advised Mr. St. John to go to Paris, the only place anyone was likely to have the money for such luxuries.

Whether that little exchange added any credibility to their mission Marshall had no idea, but it did no harm and

Davy seemed to enjoy it.

It was still a bit strange to hail French ships and have lunch with their captains as opposed to opening fire, but there was far less wear and tear on the schooner, and he felt rather protective of her. The *Mermaid* was everything Sir Percy had promised: clean, well-constructed, sailing close enough to the wind to suit even the most demanding captain.

But he was learning that the lady did not care for snow, particularly the sort that blew in like needles thrown by a capricious wind and turned a warm, sunny afternoon into a damp, icy cloud. Every time the wind shifted, the slightest movement of canvas broke the thin coating formed by half-melted snowflakes freezing on the sails, and the deck was pelted with flakes of shattered ice. He'd taken in sail twice, now, and even with only a stay-sail and the least possible canvas stretched fore-and-aft, she still seemed skittish.

Marshall tried to be philosophical about discovering his lady's foibles. They were lucky the weather had hit them when they had time to spare in their schedule and could learn how the *Mermaid* behaved in winter without endangering a mission.

"At least we're far enough offshore that we needn't worry about running aground," Davy said behind him.

"Not unless you decide to put in and peddle those trinkets," Will replied. "You were quite convincing."

"That's the point of the game, is it not?" Davy said equably. "I draw the line at going to Paris, though. When the peace fails, the last place we'll want to be is on French soil, and it's a long run from Paris to the sea."

"I don't want you going ashore at all," Marshall said. "I know you must, in the trade ports, but with luck you'll be able to do most of your dealing ship-to-ship. You should not take any unnecessary risks."

"Of course not. Really, Will, unnecessary risk is not part of the job."

"Not yet." If he were to be honest, Marshall would have admitted that the cruise thus far had been singularly lacking in danger or risk of any sort. They had sailed around the Bay of Biscay, observed the coast of Normandy, and occasionally met with another small vessel to receive instructions from Sir Percy or to pass along the record of their observations. Their first mission, despite the urgency with which they'd been sent, had turned out to be nothing more than a delivery of much-needed gold to an agent awaiting funds before he was smuggled into Spain.

If there was anything important going on with the French fleet, it would be on the other side of the country. Wasn't Nelson in the Mediterranean, watching Toulon? That was where Bonaparte's naval forces would be now, in weather warm enough to make repair and refitting an easy task. This was necessary work, he could not doubt that, but it was not the sort of job he was trained for. It was ridiculously easy.

But this new mission was different, and not just because it would involve someone they knew. This time they'd have to go right in to the French shore, where they had no business going, and send a boat to pick up a passenger. "I wish your cousin had been able to persuade his father-in-law to stay in England."

Davy shrugged. "I don't think he means to return after this, but I can understand why Dr. Colbert would want to finish old business in Paris. He left so suddenly, and for all he knows his house might have been burned down or seized by the government." He rubbed his hands together, and stamped his feet against the cold. "I hope he's found somewhere to get out of this bitter weather. He must be nearly sixty. It's natural enough that he'd want to go back and sell the house, if he can."

"I suppose so. I hope he isn't picked up as a spy."

"Why should he be? Will, hundreds of civilians have been thrown off-course by war. Dr. Colbert and his daughter were on perfectly innocent business, traveling home from a scientific conference when their ship was captured by the *Calypso*. The government gave them leave to go. They had no control over what happened."

That was true, from what the government of France knew of the affair. "Yes, but they could have gone back— and they did not."

"True, they were left at liberty in England—they could have returned to France through a neutral port, if they chose. But it was sheer chance that his daughter met and married my cousin. Once the grandchildren started coming along, it would've been foolish to take the family back to France—especially since their father's an aristo."

"You've embroidered that tale out of all recognition." In fact, the conference had been a long-planned escape for the Colberts, and it had been Kit's good fortune that they were willing to smuggle a seriously ill Englishman out of France. As fugitives from the Reign of Terror, they had never intended to return. Dr. Colbert had supported the democratic reforms of the French Revolution, but when the mob went mad he realized his country had only traded one sort of misrule for another. He'd been planning their escape since before Kit had the luck to stumble across Zoë Colbert at a friend's party, and if he had not, Davy might be poorer by one extremely congenial cousin.

"It sails near enough to the truth that no one can prove otherwise," Davy said. "And it's not as though he's the only expatriate returning to attend to personal business, or a visitor who wants to see France again. Half the ships we've passed have been English sightseers."

"And the other half merchants, I know." Marshall was not reassured. "But if we're out here, so will Frenchmen be—and I expect they're as innocent as we are ourselves."

"Very likely," Davy agreed. "That's why I made such an ass of myself peddling trinkets, you know—that merchantman seemed unreasonably interested in our itinerary." He rested a hand on Marshall's shoulder. "Come below and warm yourself for a few minutes. I can light the spirit lamp and make tea—you're chilled through."

"Soon," Marshall said. "When this wind drops."

Davy glanced up at the crackling sail, and sighed. "I'll bring it up for you, then. This feels as though it'll blow all night."

Marshall nodded absently, his mind on the ship. Night was coming on fast, and Davy was right about the weather. The sensible thing to do would be to find a sheltered cove, furl the sails, and stay put until he could see where they were going. He would have to go below, after all, to have a look at the chart.

He called Barrow over to give him the helm, and was surprised to find his gloves frozen fast to the wheel, held in place by a thin coating of ice. It broke easily enough, but he had no feeling in his fingertips. "I'm going below to see if I can find a place for us to put in for the night. Call the men down and send them below a few at a time to warm themselves. I don't want any broken legs or broken heads. We've no hands to spare and no doctor aboard."

"Aye, sir, thankee."

Marshall went below, relieved to be out of the biting wind. As he reached for the latch of the cabin door, it swung inwards to reveal Davy, with his right hand on the door and two tin mugs in his left.

"Come in, Captain! You look quite thoroughly chilled—but I am amazed you changed your mind." He held the door open just long enough for Will to enter, then closed it against the draft.

"I d-did not."

The warmth of the cabin set him shivering, and Davy set the mugs down on the folding table by the window, unbuttoning Will's ice-coated coat and wrapping him in a warm embrace.

"I only came in to look at the chart," Marshall protested.

"And so you shall, when you've thawed."

He wasn't about to argue. Davy's body made him think of tropical sands; being in his arms like this was the warmest he'd been all day. When the shivering stopped, he stepped back reluctantly. "There's no point trying to sail in this muck, not so close to shore," he said. "We'll spend the night at anchor and hope the weather clears tomorrow."

Davy handed him his tea. "Good. Drink this, I'll get out the chart."

Will wrapped his cold hands gratefully around the cup, letting the heat seep in and restore sensation. He watched over Davy's shoulder as he unrolled the chart and ran a finger along the coastline. "We should be near our rendezvous already, I think—ah, here it is. Not far."

"Yes...I thought it would be best if we were to arrive the same day he's due to signal, but with this weather I believe it's better to put in a day early. There's not much of a town there, from what Sir Percy said in our orders—we'd have no good reason to hang about." He pointed to a curve in the coastline some miles away from the village. "This should serve. We can be there by dark, and that spit of land will block the worst of the wind."

Standing close, Davy leaned against him, the curve of his arse brushing against Marshall's thigh. "Do you think the wind will be noisy enough to give us some privacy?"

Marshall's body arched toward his lover with a will of its own and his heart wanted to follow, but he caught himself. "No, I'm afraid not. In this dirty weather I think one of us should be on deck, or at least awake, as much of the time as possible."

"I wasn't talking about *sleeping*, Will."

"I know, but you're the one who said we'd need to be on best behavior."

Davy nodded reluctantly. Letting his head drop back against Will's shoulder, he said, "Yes, I did. But I didn't expect you'd set the bar so high."

"I'm in command now, Davy. I can't—it doesn't seem right—to do things I might have chanced as a lieutenant. If one of the men were to come in…"

Out of the corner of his eye, he could see Davy's eyes close, and his lips tighten. "I see. You're right, of course."

Marshall leaned down, and gave him a small but lingering kiss. "Soon. I promise."

"Of course." His face composed and unreadable, Davy stepped back from the table. "I'll go above for a bit, while you work out the navigation." He lifted his greatcoat from the hook by the door, and settled his hat upon his head. "Shall I tell the cook to hold our supper until just after sunset, then?"

"That would be good, yes. Davy, I'm—"

"Not at all, Will, you're absolutely right. With any luck, we'll be taking Dr. Colbert directly back to England, so perhaps we can manage a night ashore once we're there, and if not..." He shrugged, and left the cabin before Will could think of anything to say.

Davy wasn't being fair. No, that was a lie. He wasn't being fair to Davy. They'd had only that one night together. They were still in port the night after their reunion, but since the *Mermaid* needed to go out with the tide and that meant leaving before dawn, they had simply slept aboard, in hammocks a little more comfortable than Navy-issue, but separate nonetheless. Will wished now that they'd kept their room at the inn, but as Captain it was his duty to put the mission first, no matter what his personal desires might be. They had completed their mission, the first mission of his new command, successfully and in good time. That ought to count for something.

And he's the one who arranged all this! He's no fool—he must have known it wasn't going to be a pleasure cruise!

But far from justifying his self-righteous attitude, Will's memory threw back the times he had been willing to take chances—dangerous, foolish chances, in situations far more uncertain than this. And he did not even want to think about the chances Davy had taken for him, because that would be a reminder of the time their luck had failed. Not to mention the danger that lay in wait as soon as France and England resumed hostilities.

Marshall wasn't used to fear—not for himself, at any rate. He went into every battle knowing he might die, hoping that if he did, it would be quick. But this new fear came close to swamping him if he looked at it too closely.

It was damaging him as an officer and even as a lover. He was becoming afraid to take chances.

Do you really believe that if you don't touch him, fate will somehow keep him safe?

He had no answer. Perhaps there was no answer. With their lives always dependent on the whim of wind and water, it was no wonder that sailors were known as a superstitious lot. Marshall had always thought of himself as a man of logic, an officer above superstition, but he wondered if he had developed a delusion all his own.

If so, there was nothing he could do about it right now. The chart fixed in his mind's eye, he drained his cup and put it back in its rack, then buttoned up his coat and went back above. If they found the cove before nightfall, got the *Mermaid* riding safely at anchor, and the crew set to short rotations to compensate for this bitter weather, perhaps the wind would indeed prove strong enough to hide a little unauthorized activity in the main cabin. He'd make it up to Davy later, if they had the chance.

"Any change in that light?"

"No, sir. But she's no closer now than she has been. If it's a boat at all—I'd say not. Hard to be sure, with the fog so thick."

The lighthouse on the spit of land forming the cove had been visible as a bright, pearly beacon, the only thing visible in the fog. But after they had dropped anchor, one of the men noticed a dim yellow glow in the general direction of the shore. It could have been a light in a house, or a ship's lantern—though if that were the case, there should have been two, one on either end of the vessel, as there were on the *Mermaid*, to prevent collisions.

Their signal was supposed to be a light in a window of

a particular house, shown any time between eleven p.m. and two in the morning, and that house might well lie in that general direction. But with this damnable fog, he could not tell whether the light was in a window or somewhere else. And if it was their signal, it should be waved back and forth every half-hour. On a clear night, such movement would be readily apparent. On a night as shrouded as this, who could say?

Marshall was inclined to believe that the light came from a building of some sort, rather than a vessel. It was near three bells, one-thirty in the morning by shore time, and this was a small, quiet village. Who would be up at this hour? A mother watching over a sick child, an old man restless and unable to sleep? Or a military observer of some sort, with a telescope directed at the unidentified craft lingering a mile or so offshore?

He finally decided there was nothing he could do about it at this hour, not without sending a boat to investigate. That was exactly what he would have done, in wartime—though his own lights would be out, if he'd been sending a party ashore to spy out the land or wreak mayhem. But it would be foolish and uncivilized for a merchant to send his crew skulking about on foreign soil in the dead of night.

Marshall grimaced as he realized that his earlier good intentions toward Davy had completely slipped his mind. The wind was indeed brisk, certainly enough to cloak any small murmurings in the captain's cabin directly below his feet. But the deck-glass that refracted daylight into the cabin showed no glimmer of lantern-light within.

Davy had been subdued at supper, and had not repeated his earlier invitation. Instead, he had chattered on in his polite, social style, regaling Will with news of the far-flung Archer family, the anticipated entrance of his youngest sister into Society, the next-youngest sister's difficulty in finding a husband, his eldest brother's exasperation that, try as they might, he and his wife had not yet managed to produce an heir. It was all trivial stuff to Marshall, though possibly not to Davy, and it had at least protected them against the uncomfortable silence that would result if Will were responsible for making conversation. They expended many words over dinner, but they said nothing.

He should have said something then, when he'd had the chance, but he'd had no idea where to begin. He didn't have Davy's gift for words. When they had the schooner safely settled in, he'd decided, he would employ a direct physical approach. That would be much simpler and no doubt equally satisfactory.

And then one of the crew had seen that hovering light in the distance, and personal desires had been set aside for the time being. At last, though, everyone on watch agreed that it had not moved in all the hours they'd watched. Yes, it might have some sinister meaning, but more likely it was simply lit to guide a local home in the dark.

It was time to give up watching and get some sleep. Hoping his lover might be waiting awake in the cabin, Marshall handed the helm off to Spencer, most senior of the men on watch, with instructions to wake him immediately if anything occurred. He went below quietly and opened the door with care.

The faintest glimmer of light filtered through from the lantern hung by the binnacle on the deck above. He could make out the heavy curve of a hammock on Davy's side of the cabin, the less substantial shape that was his own canvas bed. If he held very still he could hear soft, regular breathing. "Davy?" he whispered. "Are you awake?"

No response. Whatever chance he might have had to make amends, he'd missed it.

He waited a few moments longer, wondering whether he should wake his lover up, then decided against it. His own weariness would certainly dampen his ardor, and Davy deserved better. Yawning, he peeled off his outer garments and realized that the illusion of warmth in here was only in contrast to the bitter cold above; he wasted no time in wrapping himself in his blankets and pulling them up over his head. Tomorrow. Somehow, tomorrow, he'd have to find time to ease this awkward restraint between himself and his lover. He wanted their friendship back again, the easy comfort of being together even when privacy was impossible.

He wished he knew what had gone wrong, and what he needed to do to make it right.

Chapter 4

The fog lifted at daybreak, and sunlight began to melt the frost off the *Mermaid's* railings. The light that had been so perplexing and ominous in the mist proved to be a lamp mounted beside the door of a handsome stone home built on a rise a little way beyond the smaller buildings that clustered along the beach. In a village as small as this, it might be the only light available on a dark night.

And in fact... As Marshall squinted through the glass, he realized that the grey stone and mansard roof, with one central cupola directly behind the church tower, seemed to fit the description they'd been given in their last set of instructions. "Mr. St. John," he said, handing the glass to Davy, who stood at his elbow, "does that building behind the church steeple look familiar to you?"

Davy squinted through the glass, then nodded. "I can fetch the description, but if memory serves I would say it's the home of Dr. Colbert's local contact. Though I suppose he's not a contact in the military sense of the word—call him a scientific acquaintance, if you like."

"That's something accomplished, then. We know where to look for our signal." It was a pity that Monsieur—what was his name, Beaumont, Beauville—? Beauchene, that was it—was not actually an English agent. If he had been, they could leave a message that they were in the vicinity and ready to rendezvous with the doctor. As it was, Beauchene was merely a scholar of Dr. Colbert's acquaintance, confined to his home by some sort of physical infirmity, and Colbert's visit was going to be unannounced.

"It's too bad we can't just send a message along and ask whether they've seen him," Davy said aloud. "I hope our intelligence is current, and Beauchene is still in residence."

"Indeed. But now that the fog is gone, we'd best be away. Do you fancy a run down the coast to meet one of those gentlemen on your list of potential customers?"

"Better than dropping anchor and waiting for a Frenchman to sail by and inspect our papers," Davy said. "I'd like to see if I can find anyone willing to exchange a few garnets for amethysts. We might show no profit, but that would add a little variety to my stock and prove that we really are trading."

"I've no doubt you'll have be able to open a shop in earnest by the time we're done," Will said.

"I've precious little else to do, Will." Davy handed back the spyglass. "Do you ever wonder what we will do when the war ends? I have no idea."

Will tucked the instrument into his pocket. "The Navy will still exist, even if it's smaller. When the war with France is over, there will still be Barbary pirates, slavers, and His Majesty's interests to look after in South America and the Pacific."

"Then you mean to continue in the Navy?"

"Of course, if I can. You've said it yourself—when the peace breaks, Sir Percy's interest may help me get a ship—or perhaps keep this one, though she'd need to be better armed. And it's only one step from Commander to Post Captain."

Davy smiled, though Marshall thought he seemed troubled. "So you're beginning to believe what I've been telling you about your chances for command?"

Marshall shrugged. "I don't have your confidence, but your hope is contagious. When Bonaparte comes—and he is bound to come—it's the Navy that must stop him. The man's a genius at warfare on land, but he's no match for Nelson or Collingwood. If he were as good at sea as he is on land—and I mean no offense to our own Army—I should fear for England's survival."

"Thank heaven for small favors, then."

"Yes. It's good to realize that Boney's not quite as infallible as he believes himself to be." He turned away for a moment, to where Barrow stood at the wheel, and gave orders to get the *Mermaid's* anchor up and get her under way. It would not do to linger.

Davy gazed out across the water at the village shrinking in the distance, his expression thoughtful. "Neither was Julius Caesar infallible, nor Alexander. They never are, but they always believe themselves to be. What must it be like, Will, to be consumed by such ambition? To believe that one has the wisdom to rule the world?"

"What a mind you have!" Marshall said. "But I can't imagine such self-importance. I should be content to rule one ship and do it well. I believe that such men think less of the wisdom to rule, and more of the power."

Davy shook his head. "I can think of only one reason to wish for such power," he said, "and that would be to be able to wipe out any law that makes love a crime."

Will nearly said, "And cheat the mob of the pillory and the gallows?" but caught himself. "My father once said that if he ever saw people honor Christ's word except in the breach, he'd faint from shock. 'Judge not' seems to be even more difficult to follow than 'love one another.'"

"Hate's easier, I suppose." Davy sighed. "I'm sorry—" he began at the same moment Marshall said the same thing, then he persisted, "I'm sorry I've been so cross these past few days. Having so little to do leaves me too much time to fret over small things."

They were standing at the windward rail atop the little raised section at the stern that passed for a quarterdeck, and by naval custom the crew was giving its captain such privacy as was available. They were out of earshot, if they spoke quietly, and as the *Mermaid* cleared the spit of land that formed the harbor where they'd sheltered, a steady wind blurred sound even more. "I'm sorry, as well," Marshall said "I've been too preoccupied—"

"With the ship, and the mission. As you must be."

"Still—"

"No, it's true, Will. This is not a pleasure cruise. It's not disagreeable, but we have a job to do. At least, you have a job. My role is intermittent—standing watch occasionally and playing with shiny stones when we have guests."

"Would you rather stand a regular watch?" Marshall offered. "As owner, you have the choice, and the ability, too. Mr. St. John served as navigator for Sir Percy, did he not?"

"Yes, until he was shot by pirates." Davy's current disguise had been constructed late the previous spring, after his brush with death in the West Indies; intelligence sleight-of-hand had transformed him into David St. John, erstwhile Canadian trader, to allow the traitor who'd shot him to think that his identity was still secret. "If I stand watch above when you're off-duty, you would have a little time to yourself in the cabin."

As Davy said that, his face lost some of its animation and shifted into what Marshall thought of as his quarterdeck face, bland and formal. He was drawing back, and Marshall had no idea why. "That was not what I intended," he said quickly, making a conscious effort to keep his voice low. "I am just as happy when we're in the cabin together as not. Happier."

"Yes, well...there's such a thing as avoiding temptation." Davy met his eyes and looked away quickly. "Besides, you are the captain. What sense would it make for us to trade watches if we were both on deck or below, at the same time? He lowered his voice to barely more than a whisper. "Will, if we've got to be on our best behavior at all times, that might be easier if we were sleeping on different watches."

Marshall tried to find a reply to that, but he felt as though the tangle of emotion kept him from thinking clearly, and the wind whipping at his face whirled his thoughts away. "Is that what you want?" he finally asked.

"What does that—" Davy took a deep breath and closed up completely; even his voice gave nothing away. "I think it's a reasonable thing to do, given what you said yesterday. I understand what you said, and I agree that you very likely have the right of it. All I mean to suggest is that under the circumstances, a bit of solitude—what little one has, on a ship—might be beneficial."

"I did not mean that we should avoid one another," Marshall said carefully.

"How could we? We're on a *yacht,* for pity's sake. We couldn't avoid one another unless one of us jumped overboard!"

Marshall ran out of words. From the expression on his lover's face, Davy was just as nonplussed. Why were they quarreling, and just a few minutes after they'd apologized for being cross with one another?

"Well, I mean to go below now and have a look at the charts," Marshall said. "There was no signal from the *château* last night. I'd swear to that and so would Barrow, and everyone else who was on deck. Coming by every night would soon attract attention, so we shall sail with the wind today and beat back tomorrow afternoon, taking our time so that we arrive after dark. We rendezvous with Sir Percy two days later, to deliver Dr. Colbert if we have him and decide what to do if we don't. You're welcome to join me below, if you like. I am not that fond of my solitude."

Davy looked as though he was about to decline, then nodded. "Thank you, I will. My blood must have thinned during those months in the Indies. This wind has me chilled to the bone."

"Then I'll recommend the remedy you offered me last night. Tea, good and hot."

And an embrace, at least, Marshall decided. He'd ask Clement, his steward, to bring tea and biscuits, which would give them a few moments alone together. That would not be long enough for much more than a kiss or two, but he truly must reassure Davy that the need for discretion did not indicate a lack of desire.

⚓ ⚓ ⚓

They had no signal from Dr. Colbert the following night, even though at least three pair of eyes were trained on the *château* between the hours of ten and three. By four a.m. they were on their way once more, to rendezvous with Sir Percy on the other side of the Channel near St. Catherine's Point. Marshall was reluctant to deliver his first negative report thus far, but found his employer not only unperturbed, but unsurprised. Word had preceded them, from an agent in Paris, that the doctor had completed his personal business and was on his way to the coast.

"The unfortunate thing is," Sir Percy said, "The good doctor left the city several days later than he originally intended. We'd expected him to come along the coast, but he's gone overland. I'm sure he has his reasons—and I wish I knew what they are."

"And what if he never appears?" Davy asked bluntly. "How long are we to wait before taking action?"

"It shouldn't come to that. If we don't see you in ten days at the most, I'll be in touch. We've already sent out inquiries to other sources, so perhaps we can glean something of interest."

That was not much of an answer, all things considered. This was no stranger they were discussing. Marshall and Davy owed a great deal to Kit, and they were both fond of his wife, Zoë, as well as her father. There was no question of abandoning Dr. Colbert in dangerous territory, but it was a hundred miles from Paris to the shore. Anything could happen on such a long journey, and the risks were higher for an older man traveling alone.

Given the delay in the doctor's schedule, they might have had time to spend a day in port, but Sir Percy had brought them fresh provisions along with a few pieces of mail, so there was no sound reason to delay. With a slightly frustrated Marshall at the helm, the *Mermaid* came about and headed back across the channel.

⚓ ⚓ ⚓

Four days went by, with as many night-time runs in to shore, and nothing to show for any of them. The first week of December slipped uneventfully into the second with a night of rain that left bare skin wet and numb. The crew said nothing, but they were growing restive, and so was David Archer.

He had an uneasy feeling about this mission. Yes, they had a plausible explanation to offer for their presence; Sir Percy had decided there was no harm in a modest amount of the truth. Archer had even rehearsed the tale he'd give the French captain, if and when they might encounter one. He'd rehearsed it so many times that if he were an actor he'd be afraid the role had gone stale. The story was simple: he'd received a letter from his cousin, Baron Guilford, saying that his father-in-law wanted to be met at a small village on the coast and there was simply no way to contact him to say that it would be inconvenient and not a very good idea. The old man was harmless, a bit of an eccentric, and the Baron wanted *Grandpère* brought safely home to the children. After the favors St. John had received from Baron Guilford, he wasn't going to disoblige him.

Why did they look for the signal at night? Colbert had decided it would be easier for them to be sure of his presence than in the daytime. They would not send a boat until after sunrise, of course. Indeed, Captain Marshall thought it a foolish plan, and liable to lead to trouble—Will was quite ready to speak his piece on that, and he wouldn't need any acting ability—but Captain Marshall had only been hired to sail the vessel, and since Mr. St. John was the owner, he had a right to make the decision, didn't he? After all, Dr. Colbert was a Frenchman by birth and he'd been allowed in right enough, so where was the harm in picking the old fellow up by the seaside?

If Archer hadn't heard similar foolishness himself, usually from civilians in need of rescue, he'd find it hard to say such a thing with a straight face. But with any luck at all, the covering story would never be needed. When they saw the signal they would swing a lantern with a red glass, send a boat, and meet Dr. Colbert on the beach.

All he had to do was appear. Which he refused to do.

The days passed slowly, running in to shore late and back into the channel before dawn. They were blessed with decent weather, clouds that seldom rained. Every morning, the sun would appear at the very edge of the world, sparkle beautifully on the water, then slide up into the clouds and stay there through most of the short day until it reversed the process in late afternoon.

Captain Marshall took advantage of the time to bring the crew up to scratch. The guns were never discharged; it would have been abysmally stupid to attract the attention of the French Navy that way. But he did hold dumb-show drills, running their little guns out and going through all the motions short of firing. It improved their time and gave those who had not worked together before the chance to work in teams. Target practice would have been even better, but these men, all shipmates from *Calypso* and *Valiant,* could be trusted to know how to handle a real battle.

But there was no time for him to be alone with Will. The occasional kiss, an embrace at bedtime if one happened to be in the cabin when the other was going to bed… It was like being back in the Navy again, only worse. How could one arrange a surreptitious tryst with one's lover without the Captain's knowledge when one's lover *was* the Captain, and stricter on himself than he would be toward any of the crew?

Archer finally decided to behave and think as he had when he and Will had first served together, when he was hopelessly in love with a man who had never even looked at him except in friendship.

Had it been easier then? Yes, in some ways it had. It was simpler and less painful to long for what one could never have than to miss what one had once cherished. And he did miss it. A terrible thing, to miss someone who was standing not two feet away.

"We need to investigate," Will said on the tenth of December, as he and Archer were finishing dinner in their cabin. "Unless Dr. Colbert has been taken by the French, he should have arrived by now."

"How do you propose to do that?" Archer asked. "This village—and it barely qualifies as that—is far too small for me to pretend to be looking for a jeweler's shop."

"Of course it is." Will used the last of his soft-tack to scoop his bowl clean of the thick beef soup Clement had concocted in the *Mermaid's* tiny galley. "I had two notions in mind," he said when he'd finished the morsel. "The first was that, since we have no doctor aboard, I might go ashore and ask if there is any medical help at hand—an apothecary, or even a horse doctor."

"And the other?"

Will shrugged. "The truth—the story we have that fits the facts of the matter. I think that would be the simplest and best plan, and you would not be faced with swallowing some nasty concoction for your innards."

"I would not be faced with it? Will, you're the Captain of this vessel. Since Dr. Colbert is my uncle—by marriage, but my relative nonetheless—I should be the one to go looking for him."

The look Will gave him was so fierce he instinctively leaned back. "No," Will said. "Absolutely not."

Archer could only stare. He knew that his supposed authority over Will was fictitious, but up until now they had arrived at decisions by mutual consent. He could argue or wait for reason, so he waited.

Eventually Will said, more rationally, "Davy, I'm in command—it's my responsibility. And would it not make sense for the ship's owner to stay aboard and send his hireling ashore?"

They were heading for another quarrel; Archer could feel it. He counted to ten, and then said, "Are you aware that you have just put forth two opposing lines of reason in support of a single argument?

Will glared at him for a moment, then his face relaxed into a smile. "Well, no. But would you not say that means that no matter what argument you choose, I am correct?"

"On the contrary. Whether you are in command—and should *stay* in command, aboard this ship…or *I* am in command, and should decide whether to go searching for my own relative, I would say that no matter what argument I choose, you'll refuse to admit you are mistaken."

Will sighed. "Davy, the doctor should have been here days ago, even if he did leave Paris later than we first thought. We have no idea where he is, or what has delayed him. There might be some simple reason that he cannot signal—he could be sick, or injured, and unable to get to that window. Or Beauchene might not be there any longer. If I go ashore openly, in broad daylight, ask a few simple questions…"

"And what if there are no answers? What if Beauchene is there, but has not seen the doctor? What then?"

"Then we would at least know something."

"Nothing of any use." He took Will's hand across the

tabletop, as though some physical connection would keep them from drifting further apart over this disagreement. "Will, I hate waiting, too. We can't continue to run in and out of the harbor indefinitely. I keep expecting a French corvette to appear and take us prisoner, and I don't fancy being executed as a spy."

"We'd have the codebooks over the side in an instant," Will said. "There'd be no proof of any ill-doing."

"Perhaps not. But they could hold us long enough to make the rendezvous impossible, and where would the mission be then? It's not that I am unconcerned about Dr. Colbert," he added. "I am afraid he has come to grief already, and I wish he had never gone on this damned errand."

"Do you have any alternative to going ashore?"

"Wait another day," Archer said, holding tightly. "And hope we see the signal tonight."

Will rubbed a thumb across Archer's knuckles. "Very well. But, Davy, if we see no sign, we must do something soon. Sir Percy never said we should not go ashore."

"He never said we *should*, either. And he certainly did not advise it." But Archer could see no point in pursuing the question any further. A day's reprieve was less than he'd hoped for, but at least Will wasn't going ashore this evening.

If Archer had anything to say about it, Will wouldn't go ashore at all. It wasn't that he had a death-wish, but between the two of them, from a purely military point of view, William Marshall was of more value to His Majesty's Navy. And Archer suspected that if he went and did not return, Will would adjust to being alone far better than he would, himself.

Will had managed well enough in Portsmouth all those months, hadn't he?

Chapter 5

Marshall woke early on the second morning after he'd promised Davy one more day. He had let the matter ride the day before, hoping that by some miracle they'd see the signal on the second night. But the hours had crept by with no sign, no light, and, at the end, no hope.

He had said nothing more about going ashore. Neither had Davy. It was as though each was reluctant to open the discussion, and the longer it went unsaid, the more difficult it became to say anything. Perhaps Davy thought he'd abandoned the idea, though he should have known better. Marshall had taken evasive action by going off-watch as soon as they were well away from shore; his lover had taken the middle watch and was now sleeping soundly, with nothing visible above the edge of the hammock but a gleam of tousled gold.

It was harder than he'd expected to summon his resolve and follow the plan he'd made the previous night. Sliding out of his hammock with the utmost care, he dressed quietly and carried his boots outside the cabin door before putting them on. Barrow saluted as he came up on deck. "It's a fair mornin' sir. No sign of Frenchmen—except on shore, o'course."

"Very good." He gazed off toward the horizon, where the village would appear after they'd sailed a mile or two closer. "I'm going ashore this morning, Barrow. Prepare to lower the boat as soon as we're close in."

"Aye, sir, I'll ask for volunteers." He hesitated. "Will we go armed, sir?"

"The men can take pistols, but they should not need them. They can return with the boat. I will be landing alone. I'll signal when I mean to return."

The man was too good a sailor to question orders, but he'd known Marshall since he was barely old enough to shave, and seemed unable to resist a word of protest. "Sir?"

It was one word too many. "You heard me, Barrow." Marshall knew that the ire he unleashed on the man was totally undeserved, and he felt like a complete bastard. "I am going ashore to inquire about Mr. Archer's uncle, who made an unwise decision about his itinerary. That's a job for one man, not an armed expedition. I don't propose to be the fool who breaks the Peace, and I don't intend to debate the matter with you or anyone else!"

"Aye, Cap'n." As Barrow turned and walked over to speak to another crew member, Marshall regretted his behavior. He'd never had much respect for captains who discharged their ill tempers on crewmen who couldn't answer back, and now here he was doing it himself. So much for his ability to lead and inspire his men.

He wanted to be away immediately, but there was no way to accomplish that. Instead, he called down the man standing lookout and went up the *Mermaid's* mainmast himself, as high as he could, to have some space to breathe and to scout the horizon.

The *Mermaid* wheeled as the crew below made the adjustments to bring her about, and Marshall found himself tilting out over the water. That had made him dizzy when he first went to sea, but in the years since he had come to enjoy it. This was as close to flight as any earth-bound human was likely to come, and it was his ship—his own ship, the culmination of the dream he'd had as far back as he could remember.

The vast blue emptiness above and below calmed him as it always did, and the absence of enemy ships was reas-suring. Yes, Davy was right in saying that they might wind up knowing little more after the visit than they knew right now—but if nothing else, he should be able to learn whether or not Dr. Colbert's friend Beauchene was still in residence at the *château*. If so, they would wait a little longer. If he was not—well, that would mean a fast run back to England for new orders, and the hope that there was some other agent of British Intelligence already on French soil who might be assigned to find Davy's missing uncle.

Oh, Lord. Davy.

He must be told. Marshall couldn't very well sneak ashore while his lover slept. He was the Captain. That would be a low, cowardly, and dishonorable trick to play on the man who would be left in command of this vessel. He simply could not do that.

That didn't keep him from wishing he could.

He did wait, though, as long as possible. When the houses along the shore began to grow from tiny outlines to visible dwellings, he reluctantly climbed back down to the deck and went below.

He found Davy awake and dressed, standing with both arms against the frame of the stern window, his back to the door. "Good morning, Captain," he said without turn-ing.

"Davy—"

"I heard the davits creaking," he said flatly. "They're getting the boat ready, aren't they? Were you planning to wake me, or would you have just left a note on the pillow?"

"Of course I was going to wake you. Why else do you think I'm here?"

"I could not begin to guess."

"Davy—" Marshall set his teeth. "Mr. Archer, would you do me the courtesy of showing your countenance?"

"Certainly, Captain." Davy turned, his eyes blazing. With exaggerated courtesy he executed a perfect salute, holding it until Marshall was forced to return it, then his arm snapped back to his side. "I am, as always, at your service."

Will took a deep breath. "I apologize for taking you by surprise this way, but I feel sure you must have known I would go. Two days ago, you asked me to wait one more day, and I—"

"You are in command, sir. You need not apologize to anyone for your—"

"Davy! For the love of God—"

"—actions."

Even furious, Davy was in control of himself enough to keep his voice down. Marshall was having trouble doing that. "For God's sake, you know perfectly well that we cannot continue to lurk along the shore indefinitely. We're bound to attract attention. We need information, and there's no way to get that standing twenty miles out to sea."

"Let me go instead. My French is better. Or let us go together."

"No. I'll not risk anyone but myself."

"You are treating me as though I'm the merest grass-comber," Davy said. "No, worse than that. You're treating me like a damned mistress. Is that all I am to you now?"

"*What?*"

"Do you think I am weak? Helpless? Some fragile thing that wants protection?" Hurt and anger radiated from him; Marshall had never seen him in such distress— not over something he had done. "For God's sake, Will, I was shot, not gelded!"

Marshall was startled into silence. Finally he said, "On my honor, Davy, I mean you no insult."

Some of the tension went out of Davy's posture, and he sighed heavily. "Yes, I know you didn't mean it so. But, Will, you have been watchful as a hen with one chick. You are treating me like a child—a beloved child, but not a man. And making me stay aboard while you go ashore—do you find me that much of a hindrance?"

"No, of course not." He wished that he had his lover's knack for levity, but the best he could manage was, "Christ, Davy, do you think there is anyone else in the world I would trust with my ship?"

"You could leave Barrow in command. He's forgotten more than I'll ever know."

"You're right. I know he could sail her as well as we do, and likely better. But have you forgotten? You and I are the only ones who know our true purpose. I could trust Barrow with the ship—but I could not burden him with that responsibility."

"You have an answer to every argument, Captain." Davy dropped to the bench beneath the stern window. "I concede," he said, and added ironically, "not that I had anything to say about it in the first place. What are your orders?"

Marshall sat beside him. He wanted very much to hold

Davy before he went ashore, but with his lover in this prickly state it would be like embracing a hedgehog. "I don't expect to be gone for more than a few hours. I'll be sending the boat back purely as a precaution—a waste of time, I'm sure—but I want you to be ready to run if necessary. If you see any sign of the French Navy, get as far away as you can, as fast as you can."

"And what of you?"

"I'll be out on that spit of land at the end of the cove, after it's full dark. Or, if Beauchene is there and all is well, I'll use the same signal we've been waiting for."

Davy nodded. "Very well. And what if you do not?" He looked up, and Marshall saw the fear in his lover's eyes, and thought his heart would break. "What if I never see you again?"

"I should only be ashore for a few hours," he said, knowing how inadequate the words were.

"Of course," Davy responded woodenly.

They both stood.

"Oh, by the way," Davy said. "When I collected your things, I saw—truly, I did not mean to spy—but I noticed that the letters I sent from Jamaica had never been opened."

Marshall was mortified, but oddly relieved. At last he had some idea why there had been such an undercurrent of unhappiness in Davy's manner. "I'm sorry, truly I am. I could not bring myself—"

Davy waved his hand, a dismissive motion. "I understand, we've been through this. My letters might have persuaded you to come back. And there's no need now, is there? Here you are. What I meant to say is, there is nothing so stupid or melodramatic as a letter sealed and posted and left to molder. May I have the damned things back, so

I may dispose of them?"

"No!" Marshall was surprised at his own vehemence. He was not about to tell his lover how many nights he had gone to sleep with his cheek resting on that small but precious bundle. "No, you may not."

He had been about to leave the cabin, but he took the time to lift the lid of his sea-chest, rummage in the keepsake box, and stow the letters safely in an inner pocket. "I'll take these with me," he said. "And I shall read them the first chance I get, and if you touch them I'll clap you in irons."

The ghost of a smile lifted one corner of Davy's mouth. "There are no irons on this ship."

"I'll have Barrow buy a set next time we're in port."

"You've the makings of a tyrant, Captain."

"Not so long as I have you for a gadfly."

"Will—" Suddenly Davy was in his arms, their bodies melded together, lips meeting as though it might really be the last time. He held Davy close enough to let the touch of his body impress itself all along his own. Why, *why* had he not made time, barred the door, taken the chance? What if this was the biggest mistake of his career—and the final mistake?

But there was no time to worry about that now.

Reluctantly, he disengaged himself from Davy's embrace. "I'll be fine," he said. "I shall be back before you have time to enjoy having the cabin all to yourself."

"You had better be," Davy said. "You're not the only one who can worry, you know. I tell you, Will—those weeks where you were sailing the Caribbean, wondering whether I'd succumbed to some tropical fever, I was wiling away the hours wondering if each day would be the one a load of chain-shot cut you in two. I've never felt such fear as I did when you were too far away for me to reach. It isn't conscience that makes cowards of us all. It's love."

"I will be back," Marshall promised, and left before he could change his mind.

⚓ ⚓ ⚓

Archer was vaguely aware of the boat's return, the clunk and splash as it was hoisted above. He heard the men hauling it into place and tying it down. He didn't need to watch; Barrow would handle it. His attention was all focused on the shore, where his lover was trudging up the short, sandy beach that led to the village.

The boat was loaded in and secured by the time Will turned, raised a hand in farewell, then vanished into the evergreens along the path that led to the *château*.

Almost immediately, a shout from the masthead took Archer's attention away from his worry.

"What is it?" he called.

"Something coming our way, sir. I'm guessing she's French…three even masts. Can't see any more yet."

I knew there was something wrong. I knew it, I knew it… God damn the French and all their ships to hell. But the *Mermaid* was a sleek, low vessel—low enough that the approaching ship wouldn't catch sight of her topmast over the curve of the horizon—at least, not immediately. And he could hope that, this close to home, they were looking out toward England and not in toward their own shore.

"All sails," Archer said to Barrow. "With luck, we'll be around this spit of land before they see us." After that, they could steer out toward open water, and circle back around eventually.

"What about Captain Marshall, sir?"

The breath caught in his throat as though Barrow had struck him with an axe. "Those—those are the Captain's orders. We run, and come back for him when we can."

"Aye, sir."

And if *we can.*

Chapter 6

Marshall trudged up the path, gravel crunching beneath his feet. He wondered if he had only imagined feeling the stares as he walked past the cottage closest to the beach. What did these people think of a stranger setting foot on their shore? They must have seen the *Mermaid* from time to time, these past two weeks.

The village seemed deserted. This close to Honfleur, one would expect more activity, fishing boats, something. Had there been some misfortune, an outbreak of disease? There should be children...

There was no sound but the cry of the gulls.

The path up the hill was steep, but certainly easier than going straight up the chains. After twenty minutes' steady climb, he came to a wrought-iron gate set between two stone pillars. The gate was mostly for show at this point, as the stone wall on either side had either been battered or weathered until it was no barrier at all.

He called a greeting in French, but there was no reply, so he opened the gate—it was not locked—and continued along the path to the imposing house. He knocked at the door, but heard not so much as an echo coming from within. Not surprising, of course—the door itself looked as though it was made of planks hewn from an ancient tree trunk, at least three inches thick.

After waiting for several minutes, he gave up and decided to scout around the back. If there was anyone living here at all, there should be some activity near the kitchen garden. There might be a chicken coop in back, or a dovecote.

The stone flags that led around the back were worn, but looked as though they still saw regular use. They had been swept clean of dead leaves, at any rate. Marshall followed them, and discovered a small stone terrace at the back of the house, and a discouraged, dormant herb garden. He had nearly reached the back door when he heard a click behind him—a sound he recognized as the cocking of a pistol. And *"Mains vers le haut!"* followed, hesitantly, by "Put up your hands, you English dog!" in heavily accented English.

Knowing that Davy would never let him hear the end of this—and hoping he would have the chance to hear his lover say "I told you so!"—Marshall slowly raised his hands.

Dear Will:

I hope this finds you well. I must say it is far too quiet here since you went back to sea, but no doubt His Majesty has more need of your services than we have of your company. My cousin is well, though he misses his wife very much and I must admit I feel the lack of agreeable companionship pretty severely myself.

The weather has been unremittingly glorious, and if it were not for the knowledge that hurricane season will begin in another few months—and the loneliness, and the tedium—I could call this Paradise. It was that, for a little while, but the ability to appreciate the tropics seems to have left me very suddenly, just this past week, and I would be delighted if I could ever get it back.

I hope you will be sent back to these waters soon. Please write, when your duties permit.

Your most humble servant,
D S-J

"My apologies, monsieur."

It was a friendly voice, at least, not the harsh croak of the elderly fellow who'd crept up on him with the pistol. Marshall barely had time to tuck his letter safely away when the door to the cellar creaked open. "Thank you," he called up in French. "I did not mean to alarm your household."

"Jean-Claude is easily alarmed, and suspicious of strangers. But he tells me you are a friend of Jacques Colbert?"

"Indeed, sir. My name is William Marshall, and I am Captain of the yacht *Mermaid.* The gentleman who owns her is a nephew of Dr. Colbert, a cousin of his son-in-law."

He hoped his French was adequate to this task. That mouthful felt exactly like a grammar lesson from the tutor aboard the *Titan,* although the situation was embarrassingly opposite what Captain Cooper had intended to cultivate. His captain had wanted the young gentlemen taught the language in order to converse politely with captured French officers, not to make themselves understood when the French had the upper hand.

"Yes, it is understood that my friend's daughter married an English milord. I am Étienne Beauchene. The doctor and I have many common interests of a scientific nature."

Marshall breathed a sigh of relief. "I am delighted to meet you, Monsieur. We had been told that a friend of Dr. Colbert's lived here at the *château*, and that he wished us to meet him here."

"Ah, we had wondered at your interest in our little village. Please, sir, come upstairs. Our countries are at peace, at least for now. There is no reason we cannot converse like civilized men."

"*Merci,* Monsieur." Marshall wasted no time in ascending the stairs he'd been unceremoniously shoved down half an hour before. He shook hands with Beauchene, who was much younger than he had expected a colleague of Colbert's to be. Beauchene appeared to be no more than thirty, though he wore spectacles that Marshall would expect to see on a much more elderly man. He was slender, of middle height, with pleasant features, friendly eyes behind the thick lenses, and smooth, light-brown hair pulled back in a short pigtail much like Marshall's own.

"Come," the man said. "You may leave your coat here on this rack, if you wish." Another coat, probably Beauchene's own, hung on a carved stand in the foyer, beside the front door. "And then I will introduce you to my mother."

"I would be honored." Marshall left his greatcoat, but felt its absence in a strong draft that ran across the floor when they passed a stone stairway that led downwards, probably to the cellar. As they proceeded down a chilly but elegant gallery, Marshall asked, "Have you heard from Dr. Colbert recently?"

"I have had letters from him since the treaty was signed, and I believe he has written to my mother; she has a wide correspondence. But no, I have not heard from him lately—not this past month or more. And I have not seen him. Yet he told you he would be here?"

"I wish it were that simple," Marshall said. "Dr. Colbert wished to return to France to attend to personal business in Paris. From there, he wrote to his son-in-law, Baron Guilford, asking him to send transportation. The Baron wrote to my employer and friend, Mr. St. John, who is traveling in the area partly for business and partly for pleasure."

"For pleasure—in winter?"

"Yes. He is an adventuresome man, and having bought the ship only recently, he wished to make himself acquainted with it. He has lived in Canada, so to him our weather is quite mild. And, because he is an amiable man and fond of his cousin—he is godfather to one of their children—he agreed to sail by your village and see if we could rendezvous with Dr. Colbert."

"That might cause some small awkwardness with the authorities," Beauchene said tactfully.

"It would cause a great deal of awkwardness, sir," Marshall agreed. "Believe me, I realize that, but there was nothing to be done by the time word reached us. Had there been any opportunity to contact the doctor before he left Paris, we would have urged him to choose another rendezvous. We can only imagine that he wished to visit you, perhaps to discuss some mutual scientific interest."

Beauchene shook his head. "I would be pleased to see him, naturally, and so would my mother; we do not see our friends as often as we might wish. But we have corresponded little, this past year or more—the war, of course, but also our interests have diverged. His greatest attention is given to natural science, while I have found myself more and more entertained by descriptive geometry, to the neglect of all other studies. Do you know of Gaspard Monge?"

"Descriptive geometry?" Marshall asked with genuine interest. "I have not studied it. My profession turns my attention to celestial navigation. I am familiar with the work of the great LaGrange."

"You should read the works of Monge. He was Minister of the Marine for some time, and his work on the cannon—" Beauchene broke off, and slapped his own forehead. *"Je suis fou!* No, sir, as an Englishman you should not read Monge. Not at all!" He smiled disarmingly. "I am not a man of war, Captain. I am a scholar, and when I meet a man who knows LaGrange, I cannot call him my enemy. It is seldom that I have the chance to share this passion, except in letters. We have few visitors, and I cannot travel without assistance, nor serve in the military. My eyes, you see," he added, touching the frame of his very thick-lensed spectacles. "In my home, there is no trouble. Outdoors, I fall down. In battle, I would be more dangerous to France than to England."

Marshall was touched by the self-deprecating humor. "Then there is more than one good result of your misfortune, sir. I shall never fear the chance to return your hospitality aboard ship."

"You are in the Navy?"

The question reminded Marshall that this charming mathematical gentleman was, after all, a Frenchman. "Not at present, sir. Like most of my fellows, I was set ashore when the treaty was signed. It was the greatest good fortune that my friend Mr. St. John had decided to stop dealing in furs in Canada and began dealing with gems in Europe, and needed a man with experience to take charge of his ship."

"With such a cargo, would it not be safer for him to take himself aboard a larger ship?"

"No doubt, but I believe that North America breeds men with a taste for independence. His business is small, and he does not have the large, precious stones. I have advised him that we should travel in convoy if we venture outside the Channel."

Beauchene nodded as they approached the end of the corridor. "That would be wise in any case. The war has gone on for so long that too many men have forgotten how to behave as men, not brigands. Come, let me introduce you to the mistress of the house."

They entered a large, bright room, with windows looking out onto a garden that in summer would no doubt be beautiful. The room was clean, but it had obviously seen better days; both the wallpaper and the furniture looked a trifle faded. Marshall noted all that in passing, his attention on the lady who sat in a tapestry chair beside a small fire. A tiny white dog with a brown face and huge brown ears peered up attentively from her lap. Its tail wagged tentatively as he approached.

"*Maman*, this is Captain William Marshall of the merchant ship *Mermaid.* Captain, my mother, Madame Beauchene."

"*Enchanté*, Madame," Marshall said, making a leg. He decided that he would not attempt the Continental kiss on her hand; this trim, sharp-eyed lady must have married and become a mother at quite an early age. Even though there were signs of silver in her dark hair, she appeared to be on the sunny side of fifty, and she did not look susceptible to flattery…and he did not want to run afoul of the little dog, who was watching him closely. "I apologize for intruding upon your home."

"I imagine you are sorrier still, after meeting Jean-Claude," she said in passable English. "You have made this a great day for him. Ever since the treaty was signed, he has been haunting the grounds, waiting for the English to invade and murder us all. He is good with the hens and the vegetables, but he does have his notions. And now he has caught an Englishman in the kitchen garden—his fears are vindicated."

"I came unarmed, Madame," Marshall said, spreading his hands. "I mean no harm to you or your household."

"Yet you came. Why?" She gestured at the settee opposite her. "Sit. I have told Yvette to bring tea."

Beauchene sat down beside him, and Marshall once again explained about the errant Dr. Colbert. Madame Beauchene's reaction was much the same as her son's had been. "I would be most glad to see him, but we have had no word. Why did he not travel along the shore?"

"I wish I knew, Madame. Mr. St. John is most willing to oblige his cousin, but I cannot think it a good idea for us to loiter along the coast. Our mission is a private matter, quite harmless, but our presence might alarm the authorities. Can you think of anything that would have delayed the doctor?" He included them both in his question. "He would have been traveling from Paris, and we know that he left by the last week of November."

"Jacques Colbert could be delayed by nearly anything," she said. "A good conversation, a sick child, a two-headed calf…but I do not think he would delay if he knew that you would be waiting for him. He is not a thoughtless man."

"Except for the military, travel is slow," her son said. "At least, that is what we hear. I hope he has not had trouble leaving the city."

Madame Beauchene made a noise that Marshall would, from someone less ladylike, have called a snort. "Politics. We must hope he has not had political trouble. If those fools decide to refuse him permission to leave because his daughter married an Englishman—"

"Is that likely, do you think?" Marshall asked. Sir Percy said Colbert had left Paris, but would he know if the doctor had been arrested in secret?

"It is possible," Beauchene said. "Almost anything is possible. But there have been so many English traveling to France…" He gave what Marshall had to call a Gallic shrug. "If every French family with an English connection were denied permission to travel, no one would go anywhere. We ourselves have relatives in Devonshire."

The tea arrived, and Marshall did what courtesy required, though he was becoming restless. If Colbert was not here, he should get back to his ship as quickly as possible. As soon as he reasonably could, Marshall said, "I apologize again for disturbing you, and I must ask your advice. What would you suggest I do? We should not stay too nearby if we mean to avoid creating distress, but I would not wish the doctor to be stranded here."

The Beauchenes exchanged a peculiar look. "Captain," Beauchene said, "I am afraid the only thing I can suggest is that you stay here, where you are most welcome, and wait for Dr. Colbert."

"Thank you, that is very generous," Marshall said, "but I must return to—"

"You cannot leave, Captain."

Marshall started up in alarm, the dog in Madame

Beauchene's lap yipped, and Étienne Beauchene hastily raised both hands. "No, no, I do not threaten you, sir. You are no prisoner. You cannot leave because you have no ship."

His blood went cold. "What do you mean?"

"Jean-Claude was watching when you came ashore. He told me that you had not yet reached our gates when your ship's sails fell open, and—" he flicked his hand. "Like the wind, she was gone."

There was one thing to be said for running full-out—it left no time to brood. And the *Mermaid* could run like a thoroughbred. With all canvas spread and a hull clean as a razor, she cut smoothly through the grey water at an amazing speed. Archer had taken the helm under other conditions, but this—this! If only Will had been aboard, he'd have asked for nothing better.

He called up to the lookout, and got the answer he wanted—no sign of the other ship, and no surprise, given their speed.

Barrow, standing a few feet away, caught Archer's eye. "Even if they saw us, sir, they'd never catch her." He touched the wooden rail as he said it—no sense tempting luck—but he was as proud of the schooner as if she were his own.

Archer nodded with a smile. The nagging question of whether it had been necessary to run was something to be considered later. What he needed to decide now was his next move. They were sailing west-northwest, heading across the Bay of the Seine and moving toward the point of Bonfleur. They could sail around the Point—assuming they met no other ships—or they could simply turn north, and head out into the Channel toward England.

If the unknown ship was a French vessel cruising along the shore, patrolling for foreign traffic, they'd be out of sight so long as they maintained at least sixteen miles' distance—that being approximately what Archer calculated as the distance necessary to keep the curve of the earth between the two ships. He knew Will would calculate the figure to the second decimal point, in his head, just for fun—but with no time to work it out on a slate, Archer was willing to use a rough guess.

He decided to take that chance. His other two choices were to head around Bonfleur and put into harbor, in his merchant guise, or to head out around Bonfleur on an ever-widening arc that would leave them heading toward Weymouth, on the other side of the Channel. He didn't like either option; they would both require too much time to beat back to rendezvous with Will.

North it was, then. Head out into the channel, circle around, and be ready to run straight in at night and hope to see Will's signal, hoping, too, that the mast they had seen had belonged to some English trading vessel, and Will would come aboard with Dr. Colbert and scold him for being too quick to take evasive action.

And it might not be the worst idea to tarry for a few hours at one of the rendezvous points on their confidential chart, in hopes that a messenger vessel from Sir Percy's network might happen along. It was not that Archer wished Dr. Colbert any ill—he wished him nothing but good fortune—but if there had been another change in plans or some disaster, he might need to lay plans for a rescue rather than a rendezvous.

⚓ ⚓ ⚓

Will Marshall eyed the shelf of mathematical tomes in Étienne Beauchene's study with ill-concealed envy. "I would not trade places with you, sir, but I might hope to return here, when our countries finally come to terms with one another."

"I wish you may," Beauchene said. "I have here also the *Journal* and the *Correspondence* of the École Polytechnique. It is not reading that everyone would enjoy, but I believe it would suit your taste."

"It would, indeed." Marshall could only think of how ill-timed this meeting was. If he had somehow been able to stay here for those months after the treaty had been signed, instead of moping in Portsmouth, what might he have learned in that time?

He could almost hear Davy's comment on that: *"Seduced away by a book of French geometry. I might have expected something of the sort."* But of course he wasn't seduced by it, just a bit wistful for the chance he'd missed. If he had not been in Portsmouth, he would not have been reunited with his lover, and Davy was worth any amount of theory, mathematical or otherwise. For that matter, if he had not been such a dolt, he would have returned to Jamaica and spent those months with his lover, and that would have been best of all.

Still...Davy was not here, and the books were. And so was Étienne Beauchene, who had mentioned that he seldom had visitors, and was so innocently delighted to have someone to talk to. It would be beyond rude to dive into the library and ignore such a generous host.

"If it would not be trespassing upon matters pertaining to the military," he said, "may I ask what line of this great work your own studies have followed?"

"My friend, what element of the mathematics cannot be applied to war? What part of any science is not dragged into battle? But for my part, I have taken my teacher's study of the curves of curvature, and continued the investigation. Since Monsieur le Compte was appointed to the Senate, he has not much time for his studies."

"You have much to study right outside your door, then," Marshall said. "The slope of these hills down to the sea—"

Beauchene laughed. "Yes! Poor Jean-Claude, every time I call he rushes for the line and level. He climbs where I dare not."

Something he had said a moment before set off a flare in Marshall's mind. Gaspard Monge. Appointed to the Senate? Monge of the *Sénat Conservateur,* the Compte de Péluse? "You referred to your teacher," he said. "Did you actually study with Monsieur Monge?"

"Yes, at the École Polytechnique. That was only for a little while, when my father was alive. When he died I returned home. The town is quiet now, with many of the people at the cider-house out in the orchards, but in the season of harvest I have no time for my books, except those of the orchard and presses."

"Of course!" Marshall looked more closely at the label of the bottle on the sideboard, beside the glasses they had used a little while earlier. "Calvados—I should have realized."

"Yes. This district has grown apples since the time of Charlemagne. But come, seat yourself, let me show you my studies of the slope of that hillside." He waved toward the window that looked out on the land behind the *château,* and began taking papers from a shelf.

"I should be very pleased to see them," Marshall said, but as he took a chair only a small part of his attention was interested in geometry. Did Beauchene realize what he had just said—what he had just revealed to an enemy officer? This pleasant, sociable scholar was doing research for a member of Bonaparte's Senate, the body of men who were nearly as powerful as Napoleon himself. This village might be small and peaceful-looking, but the work going on here could be used to undermine fortresses, improve the ballistics of French cannon, take Bonaparte a step closer to world domination.

And for reasons known only to God and himself, Davy's uncle by marriage had chosen *this* as the ideal spot for a clandestine rendezvous.

The French had a word for it, Marshall thought. And the word was *merde.*

Chapter 7

"I see a light, sir, but I don't much like it."

"Steady on…" Archer brought the glass to bear, but even as he did, he knew it wasn't the signal they were waiting for. It was too low, too close to the water. "You're right. That's not Captain Marshall, unless he's cut out a French frigate. Good thing the leaves are down, or the trees would hide them completely."

Barrow swore. "It's the same ship, sir. Still there. Squattin' like a toad, just inside the point."

And not likely to leave, either. Archer wondered whether the Frenchman had already sent men ashore and captured Will, or whether they were just waiting for the ship that had dropped him. Did they know someone had landed? Were they in contact with the village, or simply observing?

"Stay on course then, Barrow." He passed the wheel to the bosun, and put his own glass to his eye. They were just barely in view of the Frenchman at this point, cutting across the horizon well out of range of even a long nine. It would be interesting if he decided to give chase. Not that the distraction would benefit Will in any way. Even if he was still at liberty, he'd have no way to get to the *Mermaid* once the coast was clear.

After half an hour it became evident that so long as the schooner did not approach the shore, the French frigate was going to ignore her. Very well, then. Someone must have noticed the English ship showing so much interest in a tiny village on an insignificant strip of shoreline. But perhaps, rather than risk breaking the Peace before Bonaparte was good and ready, they were just setting a guard dog at the door. If they had seriously intended to capture the *Mermaid*, their lights would be out—or they would have waited around the spit of land and let her sail in close, then blocked the mouth of the harbor.

What was happening ashore? Had Dr. Colbert ever appeared? Was Beauchene still at the *château*—and if so, was he friend or foe? Their mission was supposed to be for the collection of information, and all he had thus far was a growing list of questions. And the questions that mattered the most weren't even part of the mission, not really. Was Will all right? Was he even still alive?

And how long was it going to be before they had an answer?

Dear Will,

I hope this finds you well. In fact, I hope this finds you at all, since I do not know if my previous letter has been able to catch up with you, wherever you may be.

Kit tells me there is a good chance that a treaty will be signed ending hostilities with France, at least temporarily. If this should happen, he has instructed me to tell you that you are always welcome here—and I can wholeheartedly second his invitation. Pleasant as England is, I do not think that sceptered isle can boast a bathing pond as delightful as the one I showed you that afternoon of your last visit. I would be delighted to return there, in your company—it was the most idyllic afternoon I can remember; I think I will never tire of that splendid waterfall.

I am regaining my strength, but am not yet robust enough to stand the rigors of a trip to England. Please, should you have the chance, find yourself a ship bound for the West Indies. If they will not let you work your passage, I expect you have prize money enough to cover the cost of a ticket (which I believe would be unnecessary—what captain would not trade hammock-space for the services of such an excellent navigator?) Once you are here I would be more than happy to see to your physical needs.

Oh, the devil with it—I have funds, my dear friend. If your savings have been stolen by some unscrupulous agent, I will pay for your passage. You need bring only your toothbrush and a change of clothing. There is work to be done here—simple transport of supplies and the like between islands, but there has been some unrest and your talents would not be wasted.

Kit is all one could wish for in a host; he is the best of cousins, but I do miss your company.

    Yours, truly,

    D S-J

Marshall folded the letter, returned it to the parchment-wrapped bundle, and blew out the candle on the bedside table before settling down to sleep in the spacious but chilly bed Beauchene had provided.

Except that he could not sleep. The ache that had lodged in his chest when he left Davy at Kit's estate over a year ago returned full-force, amplified by guilt. That waterfall... It had been an Eden for both of them, that hidden grotto behind the falls, where they had made love with a freedom they'd never known before or since. He could feel himself growing hard at the memory of Davy, naked and wet as some wild creature, incomparably beautiful in the sunlight filtering through the falling water. It all felt like so very long ago, and the knowledge that he had deprived Davy of any comfort through his own bone-headedness was hard to bear.

How could he have been so utterly stupid that he would not even open and answer his lover's letters? The longing was there in every line, and even the knowledge that Will, raised in modest circumstances, would be fearful of squandering the money he had saved after their respectable prize winnings from cruises aboard *Calypso* and *Valiant*. But the truth was, he could have paid for a ticket a dozen times over, and expense had never been an issue. It was far more complicated than that, and instead of facing the truth, he had fled. Hardly what one could expect of a bold officer of His Majesty's Navy!

Strange, how time could change one's awareness. He could see, now, how thoroughly he had deceived himself. Letting Davy go for his own good? Not really. That action had been entirely selfish, driven by his own fear of loss, with a bit of clever rationalization to make it seem magnanimous. Davy had been shrewd enough to see through that...but why had he not been sensible enough to stay away?

I don't deserve him. He said that often, and the proof was plain in his behavior these past few weeks. On the one hand he had embraced his lost love, but as soon as they were in a situation where he could justify estrangement, he had used every excuse to avoid sharing his feelings or his body.

How many times had they managed to find some quiet space aboard the *Calypso* or the *Valiant?* Even when there was little time or privacy, a few minutes was all they really needed. But aboard the *Mermaid,* he had refused, time and again, to show Davy that he was worth the risk. And he could see how unhappy his lover was. After all David Archer had done, all he had given—even the *Mermaid* herself, and the chance to save some of his old shipmates from shore-bound poverty—Marshall still seemed hell-bent on destroying the most precious thing he'd ever had.

In the chill quiet of the wintry night, William Marshall looked honestly at himself and his deeds and wondered if he had somehow gone mad from grief the previous summer, without being aware of it. So much of what he'd done since he'd fallen to his knees beside Davy's grave now seemed like the behavior of a madman. Yes, the grave had been a sham, but the grief had been real. It had been something he'd feared ever since they first became lovers, but that near miss had hammered it home.

Was he still trying to destroy their love to protect himself from that pain? It certainly seemed so.

And this situation in which he now found himself...what had he really accomplished? Trapped here, with some hulking French frigate blocking the harbor— what was he going to do if Dr. Colbert did appear? Why had he not taken Davy's advice, and simply waited? And why had he insisted on coming ashore—why had he not sent a couple of the men, to ask permission to get water or some other essential?

At least he knew the answer to that last question; he would not send his men into danger under these circumstances. In wartime, they might be taken prisoner; in this situation, they might be charged as spies, and executed. By going himself, openly and unarmed, he stood the best chance of having his story accepted. And only he or Davy could have done that, so he had to be the one.

Wide awake now, he rolled over and buried his face in the pillow, wishing that Davy were lying beside him, glad that he was not. If one of them had to be captured by the French, it was he who deserved it.

And oh, what that would do to Davy, if he were caught. To know that he had provided the means of putting his lover into danger, and perhaps to a disgraceful death as a spy. A fine reward for all his love and care.

Well, Davy had set limits on how far he was willing to go, and in a sense Marshall had deliberately trodden on those limits. He had indeed gone away again, and though he was reading the letters as he'd promised, there was no way to answer them, and there might never be.

If Davy's common sense was as good as his heart, he would realize that Marshall was genuinely not worthy of his love. If this was the best he could do, perhaps Davy really would be better off if he were free to find another— and this time he was not putting a false face of sacrifice on it. Why would David Archer want to stay with a man whose actions, in a crisis, stemmed from fear rather than love? Why *should* he stay?

Marshall threw off the blankets and went to stand by the window—not the one they'd agreed to use for signaling, but one that faced the harbor. He could see the dim outline of the French ship, and he knew that the *Mermaid* was out there, too, somewhere. He could signal from this window—but the Frenchman would see it, and know that something was afoot. Not that he'd try any such thing; it might draw the *Mermaid* into a trap, though he was sure that Davy had seen the enemy ship.

Perhaps things would look better in the morning. Perhaps Dr. Colbert would finally appear, and it might even be possible for Étienne Beauchene to take advantage of his connections to grant safe passage for his colleague and the sailor who had merely been trying to fetch him home to his family.

Perhaps it was time to get some sleep.

The Frenchmen had not moved. And Archer knew they would not move until they had determined why that small English vessel kept returning to linger near the mouth of the bay.

The other ship's presence was worrisome, but in a way it was reassuring. He had finally decided that if Will had been captured, the French captain would certainly have left a guard at the *château* and sailed back to Le Havre with his prisoner, to turn him over to the authorities. No, unless Will had gone somewhere else altogether, he was surely at the *château*.

Why had the place not been searched? Did Beauchene have some acquaintance with importance in Bonaparte's new empire that would make a mere naval captain reluctant to disturb him? If so, how was it that the man had not signaled the ship himself, and surrendered his guest?

Then again, if Beauchene accepted Will's story, he might feel that while an Englishman was an unusual sort of guest this far off the beaten path, his presence was not a threat. In fact, this far removed from contact with the larger world and tied to his home by poor health, the poor old sod might be so desperate for any company at all that Will would have to steal the silver and seduce the housemaid for Beauchene to throw him out.

And Will, for his part, would be trapped almost literally between the devil and the deep blue sea. Whether or not Dr. Colbert showed up, Will could not venture out of the *château* until the French frigate had given up waiting and gone on its way.

There was no chance the Frenchman would give up so long as the *Mermaid* kept hovering about. What Archer needed most was a diversion to bring that Frenchman out and send him elsewhere. If they were at war, that could be easily managed by sending a few men ashore with some gunpowder a little way up the coast. But the *Mermaid's* boat was too small to get men in and out again before the frigate would be upon them, and in any case this was not the place to fire the first shot of new hostilities.

There was one other thing he might try. He could go ashore at the dark of the moon, with a handful of men, and see if he could bring Will out under cover of night. That tactic stood a chance of success. The only problem with it was that if it worked at all, it would work once, and only once, and if he went in to fetch Will before the doctor arrived, they would not get another chance.

He had to draw that frigate out of the harbor. *What I really need most is another ship.*

What I really need is Will.

He stood at the rail for a long time, gazing out at the roofline of the *château*, a ghostly silhouette in the light of moon and stars. He should have taken a chance, pushed past Will's natural reticence, climbed out of his own hammock and into his lover's. He should not have allowed his resentment at the unopened letters to keep him from asking for what he knew Will wanted to give.

He should not have let that foolish, acrimonious exchange be the last conversation they might ever have.

He should not...and he would not. But he could not be in two places at once; he would need help.

"Barrow," he said to the patient sailor standing only a few feet away, "Take us out. North-northeast, show no lights until we're over the horizon, but keep a close eye for other ships."

"This is astonishing," Marshall said, delighted by the complexity of the work spread out before him. He and Beauchene had spent much of the morning and nearly all afternoon in the library, located in a room with south and west windows—to catch the brightest light, the scholar said, to help his weak vision.

Marshall had seen some of these formulae applied to fortifications, but he had never encountered the work in its entirety. It was no boast to say that Monge was a true genius. "The simplicity of it—this would save hours of calculation!"

"Indeed, it would," Beauchene said. "And the wonder of this is that Monsieur Monge developed it when he was but a student at the military academy. Before this was discovered, simply to work out the calculations for *défflement* of a fortress could take—oh, many hours longer. When he first used it, his own teacher did not want to accept that he was able to complete the work so quickly."

Marshall had asked permission to take notes, but he still felt faintly guilty at being given such valuable information. "Are you certain you should be showing me this, Monsieur? After all, our countries are likely to be at war again, and soon."

Beauchene peered at him over those heavy spectacles, his hazel eyes warm in the sunlight. "Captain, I wish that all your countrymen shared your exquisite scruples." He pushed aside a strand of hair that fell into his face. "But no, he made this discovery decades ago, and if you had turned your eyes to earthworks instead of the heavens, you would surely have seen it by now. I am betraying no secrets, and I do not believe that you are my enemy."

Marshall felt a twinge of guilt. "Monsieur, I must be honest with you. I cannot condone what Bonaparte has done, and if war breaks out again—as I feel it must—I would return to the Navy gladly. Though I must say I am extremely pleased that I would not find you yourself facing me from the deck of a French man-of-war."

Beauchene smiled. "Captain, are we alone?"

Marshall blinked, then realized that Beauchene's eyesight really was too poor to see every corner of the room. He got up and went out into the hall, just to be certain. Returning to his chair, he said, "Yes, we are."

"*Bon.* I would not want to shock Jean-Claude, or have him report me as a traitor." He reached for the bottle of wine between them and poured a bit more into his glass, and into Will's. "Would it surprise you if I say that I have no love for the First Consul? It is true, he has brought order to France—and spread chaos through the rest of Europe. He has allowed Frenchmen to behave like savages in Egypt, and there are even rumors that he had my countrymen put to death—his own wounded soldiers!—to speed his retreat from that Godforsaken region. He has sacrificed too many lives to his own ambition, and his claims of honor—p'fui! Honor? At Malta, he begged safe harbor from the Knights, and then attacked them once his needs were met."

"I know," Marshall said. "I think that may be one reason England has not returned Malta, even though it was part of the treaty to do so."

"He will pick that bone when he is ready to fight, I promise you. As soon as he has the fleet brought to readiness and the army reorganized, he will take up arms once more. And he may win, in the end. He is skilled at what he does, and completely without compunction; he would do anything for victory. To please certain influential swine he even brought slavery back to my country, after the Revolution had abolished it. For that alone I could despise him."

Beauchene took off his spectacles and massaged the bridge of his nose with two fingers. "I do not wish to see England conquer us, I do not want to see Bonaparte triumph—no matter how it goes, my poor France will be the loser. It is a hard thing, to love one's country and see it so betrayed."

There was too much passion in the man's words for Will to doubt his sincerity; outrage gave him a fire that the love of his studies did not. "But…you do military work for the Compte de Péluse…"

"Napoleon is not France, Captain, though he may believe they are one and the same. This is still my country. My family's bones lie in this ground."

Marshall nodded understanding, wondering if his own patriotism was weak. He was English, born and bred, but he did not have this deep love of any single part of the land. Of course, his family had not been so deeply-rooted; he had grown up in the vicarage his father had been given, and his family's bones lay in various churchyards in many small towns. "Your work will remain when this present trouble is gone."

"Perhaps so, but I am not even concerned for that. I do the mathematics for the joy of it, my friend. Do it I must—it is the same as breathing." He put his hand over Marshall's. "Is it not the same with you? I cannot converse with you, and see your intelligence and good nature, and believe that when you send your ship into battle it is because you wish to see men die, or count your victory in the number of lives destroyed."

Marshall winced. "I am no saint, Monsieur, but no. It is not that I seek to kill—but I have killed your countrymen in battle, and no doubt will again."

"As they would kill you, of course."

"Yes. But the goal is to capture; if a ship surrenders to me without a shot fired, I count that a victory. When I was younger, it was otherwise, of course. I joined the Navy at fourteen, and a boy needs no reason to fight the French, or anyone else. But until a boy sees death, he thinks himself immortal." He thought of Davy, and the risk that would come with renewed warfare. "As I grow older, I find more joy in sailing and navigation. I have seen enough of death. But to protect my own country…of course I will fight, as hard as I can."

"That is a reason anyone can appreciate, I think," Beauchene said. "And a man must face death for that. The war took my own father some years ago, at this season, just before Christmas. A stupid cause—his horse stepped on his foot, and it became infected. He was sent home from the front, but died soon after he arrived."

"I am sorry." Will sighed. It was impossible to think of this gentle man as the enemy, and easier to see himself as the uncivilized savage. "I wish that more of your countrymen were like you, monsieur. 'Peace on earth to men of good will...' I wonder sometimes if it is even possible."

"Could you call me Étienne? I think of you as a friend, not an adversary."

The offhand request made Marshall slightly uncomfortable, but he did feel a greater affinity for this Frenchman than he had for many of his fellow officers. "Certainly...Étienne. My own given name is William, if you wish to use it."

"*Merci*, William." The name had a certain charm pronounced "Weelyom."

Embarrassed, Marshall sought a general subject. "I think it a pity that men and nations can find nothing better than to fight one another. It seems the easiest thing is always to send out armies—could our leaders not sit down together with some of this excellent wine and find some other way to settle our differences?"

Beauchene smiled, shaking his head. "No, my friend. If we had six or eight men together, perhaps, if they were not too arrogant. But with even a few more, it would become politics, and all would be lost. Generals are seldom 'men of good will,' and politics is nothing more than war in a clean uniform."

Will smiled ruefully, thinking of the vicious attacks on Pitt, the brutal and sometimes even bloody animosity between Whig and Tory. "It's worse than war, I think. At least in a war, you know the attack will be coming from the enemy."

Beauchene slapped the table. "I knew you were a sane man! I despise war, William. But more than that, I despise politics—yes, even our own glorious Revolution. *La gloire! Liberté, Egalité,* and especially *Fraternité!* Such beautiful words—but only words. The old regime was corrupt, yes, of course it was. But the Committee for Public Safety—that was a marvel of hypocrisy. The noble words, the ugly deeds... Scarcely was the ink dry on the paper before it began corrupting itself and killing our people. The men who want power—they are unfit to hold it. I think of all lust, the lust for power is the greatest evil."

The echo of Davy's words of a few days ago was unsettling. And so was the realization that Étienne Beauchene's hand was still resting upon his own, and even more disturbing was the fact that he found that touch pleasant. "I have a friend who would agree with you," he said, trying to make his movement casual as he retrieved his hand and picked up his glass. "To friends, near and far—to men of good will."

"I can drink to that with pleasure," Beauchene said, and did. He paused a moment, looking thoughtful as a stray gleam of sunset touched his hair, giving it a copper glow. "This friend—is he upon your ship?"

"Yes. I wish there were some way for me to communicate with him, but I fear that if I were to attempt it, matters would only get worse."

"Jean-Claude told me there has been a French ship in the harbor since yours sailed off. You have seen it, I think."

"Yes," Marshall admitted. "That is probably the reason he left so abruptly—those were my orders, though as the ship's owner he could have chosen to do otherwise."

"So he has gone, and cannot return. Would it help, do you think, for me to invite the captain to come ashore and explain to him why you are here?"

If it were only that simple. "That is for you to decide, of course," Marshall said, "but I'm afraid that in the current diplomatic situation it would not help at all. I have no official papers, no permission to remove a French citizen from his own country…and I cannot hope that the captain of that ship would be as amiable a man as you are. It is his duty to be suspicious of a foreign sailor, as I would be in his position."

"There is also the problem that we cannot produce Dr. Colbert," Beauchene said wryly. He addressed an imaginary third party: "'M'sieu Captain, this English sailor is here only to take his friend's uncle back to his family.' 'Very well, produce this uncle!' 'Alas, we cannot, he seems to have lost himself.'"

Marshall laughed at the dialogue, though it was no joke. "True enough. Even worse, I have no ship to take him on if he should appear. I do wish he had made other arrangements, or that there were some way to get in touch with him."

"I am beginning to worry for him." Beauchene glanced toward the window, where the light was nearly gone. "He is not yet sixty, but the trip is long and the way dangerous, and he should have been here—what, four days ago?"

"Yes. Or even a day sooner. It's past time to take action, but I did not wish to presume. It is your home."

"I agree. We should act, then. What do you wish to do?"

What Marshall wished to do was borrow a horse, if such a thing was to be had. "I wish to go looking for him, but as an Englishman, I could not inquire along the road, so there's little hope I would find him. Is there anyone in the household who could be sent to look for him? I've little money with me, but we have funds aboard the *Mermaid* and the Baron would be happy to pay for assistance if it meant finding his father-in-law."

"That is a difficulty, but not because of money. I cannot send Jean-Claude. He is needed here, to carry wood and water for the house. The rest of us are incapable of venturing very far—and although your French is very good, you are so obviously English that you would not be safe."

"I am able-bodied, Étienne. I could deal with the firewood and I've spent most of my life on water."

"But you are a guest!"

He seemed genuinely shocked at the suggestion that a guest might pitch in and lend a hand. "An uninvited guest," Marshall pointed out, "who has put you to a great deal of trouble."

"And whose company has given me a great deal of pleasure. No, no, my friend, let us wait until tomorrow. It would do no good to begin at sunset. I will speak to our old cook. Her daughter lives in the village; perhaps her son-in-law can take leave of his fermenting vats for a day or two. Dr. Colbert has been our guest before, so it would not cause talk or suspicion if I said he was expected here."

Marshall felt his spirits grow lighter even as the room grew dim. "Thank you, my friend. I have become more and more concerned as the days passed—though I admit your library has a great power of distraction. I hope the doctor is merely delayed, but if the worst has happened it would be best to know that, too."

"We must hope it has not. Dr. Colbert knew my parents long before I was born, and we have all lost too many friends. He deserves to be back with his grandchildren for Christmas. I should have spoken before now, but I was certain he would arrive just as arrangements were made to go look for him."

"In that case, now that we have laid plans, perhaps we may expect him tomorrow," Will said.

"Indeed. Shall we set a plate for him at dinner to-night? Speaking of dinner, what is the time?"

Marshall checked his watch. "A few minutes to five. Shall I light the candles?"

"No, my eyes have had enough for today, and this room will quickly grow cold." Beauchene put the journals into a semblance of order upon the table. "Let us go down the hall and drink an *aperitif* with my mother, by her fire."

Halfway to the door, he paused and touched Marshall's arm. "William—I would not insult you for the world, and I say this only in friendship—but may I ask, are you extremely fond of this friend who owns your ship?"

"I—" Caught completely off-guard, Marshall felt the heat rise in his face. "Yes, I am, we've been together— *sailed* together, I mean—for six years." He raised his eyes to Étienne's, and added, almost defiantly, "He is my dearest friend."

"I mean no offense," Étienne said quickly.

"None taken," Marshall said, still uneasy. "Only—"

"William, I find you very attractive, and I think you do not dislike me. So…one must ask. But I think that you have your dearest friend, and do not seek another, *ne c'est pas?"*

"I—" The room seemed very warm now, and he was not so much alarmed by Beauchene's inquiry as by his own unexpected reaction. "Étienne, if I were seeking… I do not dislike you at all. Quite the opposite. But you judge the situation correctly, my friend."

"Ah, well," A quick smile touched his lips. "One must ask. At least you did not call me out for my presumption. Many Englishmen would, even those who had an interest."

"Never," Marshall said. He was suddenly full of pity for this lonely man, regretting that he could not offer more than friendship. "I am honored by your question, sir. And your trust."

"What we must decide next," Étienne said briskly, turning toward the door, "is how to communicate with your ship, once we have found Dr. Colbert."

Chapter 8

*D*ear Will,
    I know that you can write, however badly—I have seen your log entries, which is why I know that "badly" is the appropriate word. No doubt you are so busy clearing the seas of Bonaparte's minions that you have no time to let friends know you are still alive, but a line or two to reassure me of your continued existence would not go amiss.

    If, on the other hand, you are in fact no longer alive, please accept my apologies for the terse tone of this letter, and rest assured that I shall be devastated with remorse.
        D S-J

Marshall winced and put the letter back with its fellows. He broke the seal on the next.

Dear Will,
    I must apologize for the distemper of my previous letter; Kit received a long missive from home, full of news of his wife and family, and I was feeling particularly bereft. But you are the world's worst correspondent, and if there is some reason you cannot write, at least

*put pen to paper—or hire a scribe to do so—
and give me some hint of what is wrong! Did
you break both arms emulating Nelson's dar-
ing leap from one ship to another?*

*The past few weeks have been most inter-
esting, now that I am able to spend a full day
on my feet without requiring intermittent naps.
My cousin is doing excellent work with the
plantation, and I think if other owners followed his humane and enlightened example,
we would see fewer revolts and uprisings. He
has manumitted all the slaves except one very
old woman who could not possibly care for
herself, and each worker now receives a small
share (a very small share, but theirs to keep)
of each year's profit. The effect of this change
is truly inspiring. His only difficulty now is
how to deal with slaves who run away from
other plantations and seek employment on his.
If it were up to him, I am certain he would
give the poor wretches sanctuary.*

*On a more serious note, I must tell you,
sir, that the young person from whom you took
such a fond farewell on your last visit is quite
beside herself with anxiety at your failure to
communicate in any way.*

Young person? Will stared at the sentence stupidly
until he realized that Davy was speaking of his own feelings by attributing them to some fictitious young lady.
The ruse filled him with admiration. That would be a gen-
tlemanly way of passing a message to a swain if the
lady's parents did not approve of her choice and insisted

on reading her letters. And, more importantly, it would protect them both from court martial for a capital offense.

> *I hesitate to commit such a delicate matter to paper, but if you do not exert yourself to make at least some token attempt to reassure her of your continued affections, you will be responsible for a broken heart.*
>
> *I have suggested to the lady that you might possibly have found another.*

Marshall looked away. He had decided to finish reading Davy's letters as a way of reminding himself of his responsibility to his lover, and he did want to keep the promise he gave when they'd parted. Given this evening's temptation, though, the words cut too close to the bone.

> *If this is the case (and I can surely understand how such a thing could happen, since your duty might never bring you back to these shores) I believe it would be kinder for you to sever the relationship. I shall pass your message along in the gentlest possible terms, but whatever your feelings may be, I urge you to express them honestly. This silence does you no credit, and only prolongs the suffering.*
>
> *Yours,*
>
> *D S-J*

They had parted in June. The letter had been sent in September, and Will had received it when he was set ashore in Portsmouth, after the treaty had been signed. That was when he'd decided to set his lover free to find a proper life and a proper wife, and sent him a carefully copied page containing Shakespeare's thirteenth sonnet, a plea from the poet to a male friend, encouraging him to find a wife and have children.

One more letter had come after that. And he might as well read it before he slept, and complete the task. Coward that he was, he'd waited long enough—it had only arrived a few weeks before Davy appeared to set him to rights.

> *Dear Will,*
>
> *A shoemaker should stick to his last, and you should not put Shakespeare to such ignoble service. Thank you for your advice, sir, but I am not a man of inconstant affection, and having lost the only one whom I could truly love, I have no interest in seeking another.*
>
> *I wish you well in your future endeavors. I've no doubt you will make the Captain's List in record time, and hoist your broad pennant before Bonaparte is finally brought to heel.*
>
> *Should you find yourself in these waters, feel free to drop anchor at my cousin's estate. You need fear no recriminations. The young person who had formed such an attachment to you has realized that a man who would not write even a line to his sweetheart would almost certainly fail to correspond with his spouse.*
>
> *Best wishes,*
> *D S-J*

David Archer hardly needed a sword or pistol when

he wielded words with such devastating effect. He had cause to be angry, though. Marshall's negligence had been inexcusable

And yet he had come back. After such bitter disappointment, he *still* had returned, and with open arms.

Marshall folded the letters back into their cover, his mind at peace once more. Instead of his thoughts being full of a gently humorous Frenchman with exquisite manners and waving brown hair, they were focused on an irreverent, unreasonably beautiful Englishman with an acid tongue but a steadfast heart.

How was it he had allowed himself to find Étienne Beauchene attractive? He was that, of course, but Marshall had met many good-looking men without the slightest twinge of carnal feeling. He'd never felt such interest in any man besides Davy. It worried him, a little—what would he do if for some reason the *Mermaid* could not get back to pick him up? What if Dr. Colbert never appeared? How long would a handful of letters serve as a talisman against that very civilized, appealing invitation?

Forever, he decided. The notion of taking a Frenchman as a lover—even such an interesting, intelligent, and good-looking Frenchman whose dedication to mathematics guaranteed a common interest—was beyond the limits of what he could ever do. Even if the *Mermaid* never returned to this cove, he would, one way or another, get out of France and back to England, no matter how long it might take.

Only if he lost Davy would he ever think of seeking another. And God forbid, if he were ever to lose Davy, that would be the last thing on his mind. Were that ever to happen, he would die himself, in the next battle he fought. One way or another, he would be sure of that.

He blew out the candle and pulled the blankets up to his ears. He must be unusually fatigued tonight; the bed seemed colder than it ought to be.

⚓ ⚓ ⚓

Marshall woke to skies of a blue so deep and clear he knew he could not be in England. His sloop—he knew it was his, though he didn't even know its name—was anchored off a beach of blinding white sand, and further inland was greenery of a brightness and depth that made him doubt his own eyes.

It should have been a pleasant scene, but it was not, because the other ship in the harbor was *HMS Calypso,* her yardarms a-cockbill, a ship in mourning, and he could not raise a soul aboard her. He had to find Davy, but he'd no idea where to start looking. There was no one aboard this sloop, either. Where had everyone gone?

First things first. He needed to find Davy, and then together they could search for the missing crew. They had to be around somewhere.

Squinting at the shore, he thought he saw something far up the beach, near the treeline, a man-made shape, not a plant or rock. It would take too long to lower a boat, and the shore was not far; he pulled off his shoes, jumped into the water, and swam. Strange; he hardly felt the water at all, except for its chill. In no time at all he felt his feet touch the sandy bottom.

He stood and waded ashore. The shape near the trees was clearer, now; it was a squared-off tablet of stone. Marshall stared at it, uncomprehending. At first he didn't realize there was writing on it, didn't realize it was a grave marker, until the letters began to stand out dark and clear, blood-red against the pale marble: *David Archer, Beloved. 1780-1802*

"No," Marshall said. He could hear his heart thudding, his breath stopping in his throat. "No. This isn't right, this isn't what happened—"

"Will."

He whirled, and Davy stood behind him, his uniform coat open and that same bright-red stain spreading across his white waistcoat. "Davy! What— How can you—"

Davy's face was angelic, his eyes blue as the sea and his hair lit as though the sun shone nowhere else. But he was pale, white as a drained corpse, and his eyes held only pain and accusation. "Will, you left me—I waited, but you never came back, I wrote and you never answered. Why did you leave me?"

"Davy, I'm here—I didn't mean to hurt you, I'm sorry..." He tried to take Davy into his arms, but somehow he could not even cross the few feet that separated them.

"It's too late, Will." His eyes spilled over with tears. "I can't stay. You waited too long." As Marshall watched helplessly, paralyzed, Davy walked to the gravestone and lay down before it.

"Davy, *no!*"

"You waited too long, Will." He put his hand into the white sand and it pulled up like a blanket, wrapped around him, swallowed him. In a moment Davy was gone, and the stone sank into the sand, and Marshall was left standing on the beautiful beach in a darkness that would never see the dawn, convulsed with grief and loss.

The sound of his own sobbing woke him. The cold brought him back to reality. He saw the shape of the room, the rectangle of window that admitted enough light to make out the outline of armoire and chair, the frame of a picture too shadowed to see. The night was perfectly still; he had not wakened anyone with his disturbance.

It was only a dream. Thank God.

But dream or not, it was too near what had happened for any shred of comfort. And worse, too near what could happen at any time. Davy was no mistress, no child. He would not stand for being coddled or protected. If they stayed in the service together, one or the other was likely to die violently, and young.

Marshall pulled up a spare blanket that had been thoughtfully placed on a bench at the foot of the bed. He was still cold.

He busied himself with multiplication tables until the numbers ran together, then just lay staring at the window, wondering what in the world he was going to do even if he was able to get back to the *Mermaid.* Finally, after an hour or more, he passed into an exhausted sleep that was too deep for dreams.

Chapter 9

"Did I not tell you? We needed only a plan so that it might be upset."

Étienne Beauchene's voice rose above his mother's exclamation of surprise after Jean-Claude clumped into the sunny little room where they were having a light breakfast and boomed out, "Monsieur le Docteur has arrived."

Dr. Colbert followed close on his heels, and kissed Madame Beauchene's hand before planting himself wearily on a chair beside Marshall. He looked much the same as he had some years earlier—a wiry man with mouse-brown hair, now shot through with more grey than Marshall remembered. The alert brown eyes remained, though, and the ease of movement that always made him seem younger than his years. He looked his age this morning, but after such a long trip who would not? He was alive, he was here at last, and the long wait was finally at an end.

"*Bonjour,* my friends," he said, surveying the table. "Shall I speak French for the household, or English for Captain Marshall?"

"Whatever you please," Marshall said. "I am so glad to see you, sir, that you could speak Chinese and I would not care. What kept you?"

Colbert shrugged. "Bad roads, a horse that resented

my presence, and a guide with no sense of direction. I would have arrived last night, but it was so dark I was not sure of the road. I stayed in a wood-cutter's hut and made the last few miles as soon as the sun came up."

"You must have some coffee first," Madame Beauchene admonished him, passing a plate of brioche down the table. "Jean-Claude, go find Yvette, tell her we have another for breakfast, and hurry."

"Were you able to conclude your business successfully?" Marshall asked.

"Yes. My house was still my own, fortunately, and an agent had been inquiring after it. He had a client who wished to purchase the place immediately. Aesclepius must have been smiling on me." He leaned back as Yvette hurried in and placed a cup and saucer before him, and poured coffee into his cup. "Unfortunately, Mercury was less generous, so the delay to attend to business turned from one day, to two, to—what day is this?"

"The fifteenth of December, I believe," Marshall said, and Beauchene nodded confirmation.

"I have lost a day somewhere, then. Ah, well. I am here, at any rate. Madame, you are as beautiful as ever. I cannot believe you have not yet remarried."

"Nor have you, if Captain Marshall is to be believed."

"I have met many amiable Englishwomen," the doctor responded gallantly. "But I cannot follow Zoë's example and look for a mate across the Channel. There are no women in England to compare with those in France."

"Then it is a pity your stay must be so short." Was that a blush? Marshall was surprised at how animated the lady's features had become. Poor woman, she must be quite lonely here, with her son absorbed in his studies and only that dog for company.

But she went on, "For myself, I would rather be a widow and live quietly than endure Paris in these times. I am happier here by the sea with my son and my little Pierrotte than I would be with some fool in the city." Her pet, curled in a basket beside her, yipped at the sound of his name.

"He pleases you, then?"

Her voice dropped its arch tone. "Very much. It was kind of you to send him to me after I lost Antoine. I should never have found a Papillon for myself. He has been a great comfort."

A smile made the doctor's face look a decade younger. "It was the least I could do."

Marshall found himself surprised at the warmth of the conversation between the two. He would have thought them both too old to be flirting. Étienne caught his eye and shrugged. He shrugged back. Perhaps it was something in the water, or the effect of too much seaside solitude. *Oh, well,* he reminded himself, *they are French, after all.*

Then Dr. Colbert turned and asked him when they could be away, and Marshall found himself having to explain, over half a brioche and a cup of rapidly cooling coffee, why they were not going anywhere for the present.

Colbert was no happier about it than Marshall himself. "It would be better if we did not stay," he said. "Safer for these good people. I believe I was followed from Paris."

"By whom?" Étienne asked. "Why would anyone follow you?"

Colbert spread his hands. "I cannot say. Perhaps thieves, not knowing I sent a bank draft from Paris to London after selling the house. It could even be that Bonaparte's police thought me a suspicious character.

Captain Marshall, I think we would be wise to leave to-night, even if we only go on to the next town along the coast."

"Oh, no!" Madame Beauchene exclaimed. "You have had no time to rest!"

"I assure you, my dear, I would prefer to stay, but I am most concerned for your welfare. Perhaps you might visit me in England?"

Marshall sensed something afoot, but was not sure what Dr. Colbert was up to. "Sir, unless you have some other means of crossing the Channel, I would rather not travel too far. This is where I came ashore, and this is where the *Mermaid* will be looking for us. Given the profile of the shoreline, even a few miles might mean we would be left to find our own way home, and my ship would be more likely to come to grief trying to find us."

Colbert nodded. "I see. Well, then, what would you suggest?"

Davy would be out there, Marshall could be sure of that. And now that the waiting was finally done, he was more than ready to act. But, remembering Étienne's wariness of the previous evening, he took the precaution of making sure Jean-Claude was nowhere near enough to eavesdrop.

He returned to the table, put his knife and fork on either side of his plate, so that the utensils stuck out to form curves. "Imagine this is the coastline and this space here the cove. The French frigate is over at this point. She cannot be seen from the open sea, but neither can she see around the point. If we can obtain a small boat—as small as possible, just big enough to hold the two of us and a sturdy enough to rig a sail—we might strike out from the shore after dark, before the moon has risen. We could row out into the Channel at a shallow angle, away from the frigate, until we are clear of the land, and raise our sail once we were out of sight. Have you any knowledge of boats?"

"Only as a passenger, but I can surely row. And if you tell me what to do, I will follow your orders. But we cannot row all the way across the Channel..." He glanced at Marshall, obviously reaching the limits of his knowledge. "Or would that be possible?"

"We might sail across. In summer, surely. At this time of year it would be a dangerous and uncomfortable journey. But I think the *Mermaid* would find us sooner than that."

"How?"

"Since we never saw your signal, we made other plans and set points at which to rendezvous before I came ashore. Your nephew will not be wasting his time, sir; so long as that French frigate guards the bay, he will return to those points at least once every day."

Colbert nodded, sipping his coffee. "You are correct, Captain. It seems we must find a boat."

"I must also check the tide-tables. The moon is waning, so it rises late, near midnight. It would be best if we sail when the tide is ebbing, or at least not on the rise."

"I have such tables in my study," Étienne said. "I think you may need to wait a day or two for the tide and darkness together. And I do not say that only because we would prefer to keep you here a little longer."

Marshall smiled ruefully. "I fear we may be here for some time, until we solve the difficulty of a boat."

"There is no difficulty with a boat in itself. Many men in the village have small craft for fishing or trade—you saw them when you arrived, no? The difficulty is a boat that will not be seen. To take one of them from the beach and carry it away without attracting notice, that is where the thing becomes complicated." He put down his napkin and rose. *"Maman,* you must excuse us for now. Come, my friends, let us go study the tide-tables and consider this matter of a boat."

"What of your father's toy boat?" she asked suddenly. "Would that not do?"

"Pardon?"

"When you were a boy your father would take us out on the sea, just the three of us, in the boat he called his little toy." She smiled reminiscently. "It was very small. He could steer it by himself with a rope to move the sail and the stick at the back. Do you not remember? You used to love that boat."

"The skiff?" Étienne seemed surprised. "Do we have that, still?"

"I have not seen it in years, or thought of it, and cannot say where it might be. But there were times, when the war had gone on for so many years, he would tell me we should take out the old boat and sail away together." She turned to Marshall. "Captain, it has been twenty years and more since I last saw this boat. If it is still somewhere about, it may require much repair."

Marshall was almost afraid to hope, but he had to, and he could feel his pulse beating faster. "If it was put away sound, and safe from the woodworm, Madame, it might be ideal. Monsieur Beauchene?"

Étienne nodded. "We can look in the outbuildings. I think it would be best if we search by ourselves, and call on Jean-Claude only if he is needed to help in transport. I will need your assistance, Captain—the outbuildings are so dim I could not find it by myself."

"With pleasure, sir."

As they donned their greatcoats, Étienne smiled. "I must ask you to let me take your arm," he said apologetically, "for I am not so sure-footed out of doors."

"Of course," Marshall said, hoping his self-consciousness was not evident. His host did nothing that would embarrass either of them, and as they walked down the sloping path toward the road and outbuildings it was clear that the request had been a perfectly reasonable one. The path was uneven and steep in places, and even with excellent eyesight the footing was treacherous. He felt ashamed for his momentary anxiety but soon forgot his feelings in the anticipation of the hunt. At last, a reason to get out of the house, and perhaps a chance at escape!

They found it in the carriage-house near the gate, the first place Étienne had suggested they look. The original structure, built to waist-height of local stone and timber above, contained an old-fashioned coach, a lighter open carriage, and a pony cart.

"That was mine," Étienne said. "The pony is long gone, alas, and Jean-Claude has a mule who pulls the cart to market. Apart from that we keep only a pair of carriage-horses now. Come, let us look on the other side."

At some point in the past, the building had been expanded by adding a three-sided shed to the north wall, and they found the boat there, pushed to the back of the space and half-hidden by barrels, odd pieces of lumber, and various gardening tools. Marshall cleared away the clutter as quickly as possible while Étienne sensibly kept out of the way, sitting on a half-barrel outside the doorway.

"Will this be sufficient?" he asked.

"Perfectly, so long as she's sound." The skiff was small indeed—tiny, as Madame Beauchene had said, only about a dozen feet long. But that was big enough, and her size would make the task of getting her down to the water considerably easier—as would the vehicle that she rested upon, an old carriage frame with two long beams, one on either side, to support the hull. Marshall found an old hammer hung on a nail in n the shed wall, and went over the skiff plank by plank, checking her for soundness. He found a few spots around the upper edges that he was not entirely happy with, and some weathering was visible on the brass oarlocks. But her wood seemed solid, right down to the oars wrapped in oiled canvas and lying across the seats.

"I admire your father's foresight, Monsieur," Will said at last. "If he had been given the chance, I believe he really could have put out to sea at any time he wished. She's a pretty little thing."

"Very good," Étienne said, "and now for the tide-tables."

Dr. Colbert was in Madame Beauchene's parlor as they walked past, sitting close and engaged in a quiet, earnest conversation. Not wanting to waste the time the older folks had left to spend together, the two men went back to Étienne's study, where the tables told them that tonight should give them time enough, though the following night would be better.

"I would prefer to try tonight," Marshall said. "I saw no sign of anyone while we were outdoors, but if Dr. Colbert believes he was followed, it would be best to take no chances."

"If you must," Étienne said. "I agree, it is probably the wise thing to do. He may be right about Bonaparte's police. One does not accumulate so much power without also accumulating enemies."

The doctor's concern for the Beauchenes' safety had infected Marshall. "I hope we've not brought trouble to your door."

"I cannot believe you have. Yes, to meet a boat here on the quiet shore is not the proper way to leave the country, but this is a private matter. A mistake it may be, but no great crime. I can even swear that you came unarmed."

"If that persuaded you of my good intentions, I'm glad of it," Marshall said, "though I confess I wish I had my sword at hand. Still, with luck we'll soon be away and you'll not have to swear at all."

Étienne closed the pamphlet of tide-tables. "I know that we will see war again, William, and I wish that were not so. I would invite you—yes, and your friend—to visit here for a time when the circumstances are more agreeable."

"I hope that we can do that someday," Will said. "And if you enjoyed sailing when you were younger, perhaps we can take the skiff out to sea once more."

"Perhaps." But his tone said plainly, *We will never have the chance.*

It did seem unlikely they'd meet again, with the full force of war ready to waken at any moment. In the quiet of this orderly room Marshall imagined he could feel the winds of battle blowing from far away, the other wall of the hurricane drawing ever closer. "I think the Peace will hold at least until Christmas," he said. "Winter is a bad time to begin a war."

"Is there ever a good time?"

"That depends on whom you ask." Marshall shifted in the comfortable chair, wishing that it were night already so that he could put their plans into motion. He might envy Étienne his peaceful, studious life, but he was not built for this sort of inaction. It was easier to sail into battle than to linger in the doldrums of endless uncertainty.

But the day dragged on, and he had nothing to do until twilight, when he, the doctor, and Jean-Claude would use the dim light to move the skiff down to the shore on the opposite side of the point. Once they had the boat in the water, they would return to the house for dinner, and then a few more hours wait until it was fully dark and the tide was nearing its height.

It seemed the doctor's appearance had convinced Jean-Claude that Marshall had spoken the truth and was that rare creature, a good Englishman. Or perhaps he was merely looking forward to getting the foreigner off French soil—either way, Marshall was pleased to have his help.

After all the days of waiting, the few remaining hours should have passed quickly. They did not. At Étienne's suggestion, Will went up to the highest window of the *château* with a telescope and tried to see if he could spot the *Mermaid* somewhere on the horizon, as he had done a few times during his stay.

The attic level of the *château* was more than twenty feet above the ground, which, with the elevation of the hillside, gave him a vantage point immensely higher than the French frigate's. The clouds had dissipated earlier in the day, and his view out over the ocean was clear and unobstructed.

But the *Mermaid* was nowhere to be seen. Had Davy perhaps given up hope and gone back to report the development to Sir Percy? Or had he had decided to stand even farther out, to avoid being noticed by passing ships?

That did not matter. Davy would keep to the rendezvous, no matter what, just as Marshall himself would if their positions were reversed.

⚓ ⚓ ⚓

With the *Mermaid* standing in just behind the edge of the cliff that jutted out into the sea on the side of the harbor farthest from the *château,* David Archer made one last, careful check of the chart. It would be worse than pitiful to set such a careful plan only to run the *Mermaid* up on some unexpected reef.

But he would not make such a mistake. After days of anxious anticipation, they'd received word that Dr. Colbert had been seen half a day's journey away. He would be at the *château* by now, if he was ever going to arrive— and if he was not, it was high time to bring Will back aboard. A bit of outside distraction, enough to lure the French frigate out of the way, and he would swoop in, send a boat out for Will and the doctor, and be away before the slower vessel could return.

The distraction was out of his hands, now. All he could do was wait.

He'd never developed the habit of biting his nails. It was an unsuitable sort of habit for an officer or a gentleman, and given how easily tar got onto everything, it would be damned unpleasant.

It might have helped, though. Almost anything might help.

No. Nothing would help but an end to the waiting. And nightfall was still hours away.

Somewhere in the long days of waiting, Archer had decided he would be going in himself, in command of the boat crew. No doubt Barrow could have handled it well enough, and no doubt Will would be furious.

That was too damned bad.

Will had made a lot of decisions about who was to go ashore on this expedition. But he had never asked Archer to promise to stay aboard the *Mermaid,* and Archer had never volunteered.

If you didn't want me coming to get you, Captain Marshall, you never should have gone ashore alone.

Seven p.m.

The sun had set, some of the lights in the village had already begun to wink out as people settled in for the night. It was time to see if the plan would succeed.

Marshall and Dr. Colbert donned their coats in the foyer of the *château*. They had taken the boat down, a tremendous struggle in places where the weeds had grown over for years, but shoving the boat down through the undergrowth had cleared the path well enough.

The doctor was speaking quietly to Madame Colbert in the hallway; Étienne took Marshall's hand. "I wish I could come down to see you off," he said, "but with these eyes, I might never find my way back up again."

"It's better you stay inside where it's warm." Marshall clasped his hand. "I cannot say I wish things were otherwise," he said. "To have one friend I love is more than I had ever hoped for. But if things had been different..."

"Perhaps I too will find such a friend," Étienne said. "But there are many sorts of love." He pulled Marshall into an embrace—a friendly one, no more—and kissed him lightly on either cheek. *"Adieu, mon ami."*

The door swung open, admitting a gust of damp, chilly wind. And there, on the broad stone porch, stood five men. One held a lantern; the other four had pistols.

They pushed their way into the foyer, uninvited. The oldest in the group, a sour-faced, thick-bodied fellow, said, "Monsieur Beauchene?"

Étienne inclined his head. *"Oui?"*

"I regret that I must arrest you, in the name of the First Consul, on a charge of espionage and treason."

Chapter 10

"I beg your pardon!" Madame Beauchene stepped forward, the smallest of them all, cradling her dainty little dog in her arms and somehow all the more formidable for that—perhaps because the dainty little dog's teeth were bared in a low, rumbling snarl. "What insanity is this?"

"Madame," the spokesman said, "I am Captain Ulrich duPont, of the national police. We are under orders to follow a suspected spy and arrest whomever he might contact."

"We have no spies here," she said indignantly.

"Madame, this man—" he pointed to Dr. Colbert, "has been behaving in a manner of the greatest suspicion. For no reason, he has traveled a great distance to this—forgive me, this place of no importance—"

"This 'place of no importance' is my home," she said. "Dr. Colbert has been a friend of this family since I was but a girl. He came here—" she held her hand out defiantly, displaying a small ring—" to ask for my hand in marriage!"

"*What?*"

Marshall caught himself, but it was too late. DuPont's slightly bulbous eyes turned his way. "And this *Englishman*—is he also a suitor?"

"Of course I am not." Marshall stamped hard on his

impulse to laugh at the bizarre circumstances. After all the time he'd spent racking his brain for the doctor's reason in coming here. But though the situation might be ludicrous, there was no humor in the guillotine. "Captain du-Pont, I am here because my employer, a relative of Dr. Colbert, received a letter requesting that he meet his uncle here."

"For what reason?"

"To take him home to his family in England, I presume. The letter did not explain his reasons, and there was no way to contact him and ask him to travel by a more conventional route. I swear to you upon my honor, we did not come here for any purpose other than to fulfill this family obligation." That was true for his purpose in coming to this precise spot, at least.

"Your name?"

"William Marshall."

"Royal Navy?"

"Not at present. I sought private employment after being released from active service, after the Treaty."

"And your employer?"

"David St. John, a Canadian trader, aboard the schooner *Mermaid* out of Plymouth. "

"And where is this schooner?"

Since he could not produce the *Mermaid*, Marshall decided to stick to the truth. "We were not certain that this rendezvous would be looked upon with favor," he said carefully, "and when I came ashore to find the doctor not yet arrived, Mr. St. John must have left to avoid just this sort of difficulty with your Navy. I am not certain where my ship is at this time."

DuPont glanced at one of the others, who nodded. "This agrees with what we know from the captain of our ship that has been guarding this place," he said. "We shall investigate your claim, and if what you say is true, you will be released. But I must also place you under arrest."

"Monsieur, I am certain that my employer's uncle is telling the truth—"

"Indeed I am," Colbert put, shifting so that he stood between Madame Beauchene and the intruders.

DuPont regarded him scornfully. "Doctor, we have questioned many people in Paris, and I assure you, we know you were not there for purely personal reasons. My instructions are to arrest you, and anyone you may have contacted. Madame, you may remain here in your home if you wish, for the present, but in the morning I will return to Paris with these men in custody."

"In the morning! And I am to welcome you as guests in my home all night?"

"Not at all. You may have your servants pack such things as your son may need, and bring them down to the harbor. These prisoners are going aboard the ship that awaits us below, and we sail for Paris on the morning tide."

Madame Beauchene said a word that a lady of her refinement should not have known, and stalked off down the hall. When she was clear of the line of fire, Will gauged the distance between himself and the armed men. No good. If duPont's accusation was true, the doctor might be useful in a fight, but Étienne was as vulnerable as his mother, and he was in the midst of things.

Étienne spoke at last. "Captain duPont, I realize that this situation is extremely peculiar, but I assure you, there is no evil afoot. I have been engaged in mathematical studies on behalf of the Compte de Péluse, of the Senate—"

"Monsieur, your connection is known, and your loyalty is not in question. Indeed, it was fear for your safety that caused me to bring such a force—to rescue you if need be."

"You can see I did not require it."

"That is problematic, m'sieu, but your mother's social connection with Colbert will be taken into consideration. Still, you must not be perceived to be above the law. You will be allowed to denounce these two and be exonerated, but until then—"

"Denounce them!" The crack of anger in Étienne's voice was like a pistol shot; Marshall had not expected such vehemence. "Before God, I will not! You cannot expect me to perjure myself for your perceptions—these men have done nothing!"

"As you like. If you wish to make friends of spies and Englishmen it is your neck. Come, there is nothing to be gained by delay."

The door was swung open again, and Marshall automatically offered Étienne his arm as they were herded down the walkway to the beach. It was as dark as he had hoped it would be, with only the dim starlight reflecting on the white stones that marked the edges of the path. Had these agents of Bonaparte been watching the house all afternoon? Did they know where the skiff lay concealed in the wooded inlet on the other side of the point?

He had to hope they did not, and that he and Colbert could overpower five armed men long enough for them to get Étienne away. Once they were aboard the French ship, all hope would be gone.

"Arrêt! Nous avons des pistolets!"

Everyone froze, including Marshall, who would know that voice anywhere but could not believe his ears until

Davy said, "Will, get their weapons, would you?"

Dr. Colbert had Étienne's other arm; Marshall released him with a gentle push toward the doctor, just as duPont whirled and fired at the sound of Davy's voice.

White-hot rage flamed through Marshall. He threw himself on the Frenchman without thinking, wanting nothing more than to pound him through the gravel path and into the earth. DuPont struggled—it seemed as if he was trying to get to some other weapon, possibly a knife, but Will's knee pinned the Frenchman's hand. He grabbed the man's shoulders and banged his head against the ground until duPont stopped moving. He stopped himself then—not because he wanted to, but because he knew that killing the bastard could be the spark that re-ignited the war.

From the furor around him, it sounded as though everyone had leapt into the brawl, and then it was quiet. Marshall closed his eyes, took a deep breath, and said, "Mr. St. John?"

"At your service, sir." Davy came up behind him, close enough that when Marshall leaned back on his heels, his shoulder touched Davy's leg. "I hope you didn't kill him."

"No, he's still breathing." Marshall stayed where he was, enjoying that casual contact. It was dark enough that no one could see. "Are you all right?"

"Oh, certainly, it's only a scratch."

His heart stuttered. "You're hurt? The doctor can—"

"No, Captain." A quick squeeze on his shoulder belied the formal address. "Literally a scratch. He missed me completely, but they've some damned fierce bramblebushes here. How many did you see? I counted six."

Will climbed to his feet, made out the dim shapes of

Étienne and Dr. Colbert, who both seemed unharmed. "We only saw five."

"They left a guard outside. He's trussed up in the shrubbery." Davy turned to one of his men. "Owen?"

"We've got 'em all, sir. Alive, like you said."

"Good. Awake?"

"Two are."

"Tie 'em up and bring them along." In an undertone, he said, "We'll have to find someplace to put them, something they can't get out of in a hurry. Will?"

"I don't know. Just a moment—Monsieur Étienne Beauchene, this is David St. John, my employer and friend."

"I had guessed that," Étienne said wryly, offering his hand. "It is good to meet you at last, sir. We have a winecellar that can be locked from without, and should serve. What are your plans?"

"Escape, of course. From the sound of things, you may want to join us." He embraced Dr. Colbert, raising his voice a bit to be sure their prisoners could hear. "Uncle Jacques, are you all right? How could you have caused us such confusion? We would have met you in Le Havre!"

Under Colbert's loudly expressed apologies and explanations, Davy turned to Marshall. "A diversion will shortly commence. Would you care to take command?"

"Not in the least, sir. It's your expedition. How did you get here?"

"Around the blind side of the point after nightfall in the boat, then up through the woods. Barrow will bring the *Mermaid* in to pick us up as soon as the frigate's chased Sir Percy over the horizon." Davy grinned. "Percy's holding a revel on his yacht, the fireworks are

meant as entertainment, and he's got some French digni-
tary or other aboard, so when the frigate catches him,
they'll have to let him go. He does that bird-witted aristo
act so very well. Is that your dinghy below?"

"Yes, and I'm afraid we'll need it. It isn't just me and
the doctor, now. We've got to take Monsieur Beauchene
with us—he was arrested for associating with the doctor—and Dr. Colbert's fiancée."

"His—his *what?*"

"And her dog, as well. I don't think she'd leave the
little fellow behind, and it would take a braver man than I
am to ask it of her."

Marshall congratulated himself. For the first time in
longer than he could remember, David Archer was ren-
dered speechless. But then the explosions started, somewhere on the other side of the *château.*

"That's our diversion," Davy said. "We'd better
hurry."

⚓ ⚓ ⚓

The next half-hour took on the mad, organized chaos
of a ship's deck during a battle. Madame Beauchene met
them at the door with an antique pistol and Jean-Claude
brandishing a musket that probably dated back a hundred
years, but she happily put the artillery aside when her fi-
ancé explained that the gunfire was caused by an English
ship sending off signal rockets to lure the French frigate
out to sea. Will went off with Beauchene to help him get
his papers together, and Archer supervised the incarcera-
tion of their prisoners.

He shook their leader awake once his men were safely
locked in the wine cellar. "Sir, I understand you meant to
arrest my uncle."

"Your uncle," said duPont, "is a spy, and should be executed."

"Those are harsh words, sir, and I think you are mistaken. Still, I will take him out of your country and he will not trouble you again. Madame Beauchene has asked to accompany my uncle, so I will take her as well. Her son said he ought to stay here at the *château*. He claims to have a friend in the government who can clear up this misunderstanding."

"Misunderstanding! It is a crime! Your government will hear of this—sending its agents to attack the official police!"

Time to lay the false trail. "Sir, I am sorry we meet under such difficult circumstances, but Mr. Bonaparte will have to shout himself hoarse to be heard all the way to Canada. I never came here to attack the official police, but my cousin would take it very ill if I allowed anyone to chop off her father's head. I don't plan to linger on this side of the Atlantic—Europe is too exciting for a peaceful man like myself."

He had no idea if the furious Frenchman would believe him, but he knew that David St. John would soon cease to exist in any event. "By the by, I've decided to take Monsieur Beauchene along despite what he says. We'll set him ashore wherever he wants to go, but you might tell the captain of that frigate that we have the Senator's friend aboard, and he should think twice before firing on us."

The look of uncertainty on duPont's unpleasant face was a lovely thing. Was Beauchene an escaping criminal, or a hostage? Archer had a fair notion that it would take someone well up duPont's chain of command to make that decision. Confusion to the enemy!

"We've tied up Monsieur Beauchene's servant," he added. "He should be able to work himself free eventually, and he'll come down and release you. In the meantime…well, it is a wine cellar, you may as well drown your sorrows." He nodded to Spencer, who hoisted the trussed-up officer to his feet and pushed him in with his men.

Archer locked the cellar door and met Will at the top of the stairs. "Are you ready?"

Will looked flustered. "I'm sorry—I need a few men to carry some papers."

"What?"

"Mathematics, Davy. Wonderful stuff!"

For an instant, Archer was afraid Will was going to elaborate on just how wonderful it was, but he stopped himself and explained, "Beauchene's research. He cannot just leave it behind."

There was something not quite right in Will's manner—if Archer had been inclined to suspicion, he'd have called it guilt. Or perhaps it was just Archer's own seldom-felt jealousy; Beauchene was very handsome and clearly fond of Will. "Is it worth the trouble?"

"Very likely. And—he was helping us escape, Davy. He refused to denounce us to the state police. That is worth some consideration, surely."

Choosing not to borrow trouble, Archer rolled his eyes and called for Korthals and Spencer to go assist Captain Marshall. "Some papers" turned out to be two stout chests full of books and other material that Beauchene apparently could not live without. His mother, in contrast, was already standing by the front door with a small case, her maid, and a covered basket that emitted the occasional muffled yip.

"Madame, I am impressed with your efficiency," Archer said.

She regarded him from under the hood of her cloak, with an expression that was almost a smile. "Young man, I have reached an age where I know what is truly important."

He felt as though he had stumbled into a fairy tale, where the magical old woman was about to impart some precious secret. "And that is?"

"The only things of any value are those creatures whom you love, who love you in return. All else can be replaced."

He caught his breath at the strangely appropriate remark, then bowed to kiss her hand. "Thank you, Madame. I have found that to be true."

"Then you have learned it younger than most. Some never do. Shall we go, Monsieur?"

The scramble down to the cove was not something that Archer would have wanted to try again, not with civilians in his care. Dr. Colbert attended Madame Beauchene with the greatest attention, Will kept her nearsighted son from breaking his neck on the steep slope, and the maid Yvette was handed over to the tender care of the Owen twins. The rest of the *Mermaids* were stuck hauling those damned trunks.

The Owens sloshed knee-deep into the icy water, bringing the skiff close enough for Madame Beauchene, Dr. Colbert, and her maid to step into from a rocky outcrop. Klingler volunteered to pilot that boat; he said he'd run a skiff as a boy that was its spitting image. Four passengers—and one small dog—was about the limit of its capacity.

The rest of them squeezed into the *Mermaid*'s boat.

Beauchene was not a bulky man, so the boat's trim was easily balanced; he was agreeable to being squeezed in between Will and Archer. But his dunnage... Archer was not entirely happy about those trunks. Besides being heavy and awkward, their contents might cause French Intelligence to be extremely upset when they learned that Monsieur Beauchene had taken so much of his work with him. That known theft might transform this little escapade from a family rescue to an international incident.

On the other hand, if it was significant information, Sir Percy would be pleased. And if they could somehow arrange a safe return for their 'hostage,' research and all, that would be even better. Beauchene's status and his trunks were a problem for another day, and a matter for the diplomats. For now he had Will back—that was the important thing.

Except...he wouldn't have Will back, would he? Not for a day or two, at least, until they could rendezvous with Sir Percy. They would have to give their cabin to Madame Beauchene and her maid... and where the devil were they going to put two more passengers? For that matter, where were they going to put themselves?

That, obviously, was a matter for the *Mermaid's* captain to decide.

⚓ ⚓ ⚓

"I see how it is that you love him."

Marshall glanced up from his log entry to see that Étienne had come into the Captain's cabin without a sound. Davy was on the deck of Sir Percy's yacht, and most of the *Mermaid's* crew was busy transferring Étienne's dunnage and the other passengers.

They were alone together for the first time since Marshall had returned to the schooner; it had been crowded as Noah's Ark, and they'd wound up taking a few hours' sleep in hammocks slung above their provisions, in company with all the off-duty crewmen.

The *Mermaid* had made good time beating back across the Channel, even with her additional burden. Although Marshall had hoped to have some time to speak to Étienne in private, there had been no time. They had shared a meal, along with Davy, Dr. Colbert, and Madame Beauchene. It had been a pleasant occasion, but hardly an opportunity for honest conversation.

"I'm glad you do," Marshall said, warmed by his generosity. "I do not believe I could live without him."

"He could be another Bonaparte. That rescue... *formidable.* He has such courage—he would walk through fire for you. If I did not love you so much I would be jealous. But how do you keep away the fear?"

Marshall winced. Fear had been a constant companion; every night brought some variation of the Kingston nightmare. "Thank God he hasn't the ambition to be a Bonaparte. He's far too reasonable. As to the danger, the fear..." He sighed. "I wish I knew how to keep it away. I wish I could. Every day..."

Étienne closed the distance between them. "If you ever find you must live without him—and he is a beautiful man, I wish him long life—please think of me." He stooped to place a quick, gentle kiss on Will's lips—the sort one might give a brother, or a friend. "I shall go now. Please, stay here, or I should find it too difficult to leave."

Marshall took his hand. "Étienne. If a sailor's blessing has any power... I hope you find your heart's desire." Overcoming his shyness, he dropped a kiss upon the Frenchman's hand.

"I, too." Étienne smiled. "But not at the cost of another's life. *Adieu, mon cher.*"

The door closed quietly behind him.

Chapter 11

For the first time in longer than he could remember, William Marshall looked forward to Christmas with high anticipation. He had his own ship, the salary of a Commander in His Majesty's Navy, and he had even, out of the *Mermaid's* operating budget, been able to allocate a few pounds for a Christmas treat for his crew. It wouldn't be much, but roast goose, plum pudding, and fresh vegetables were rare enough aboard ship, even in this season.

The feast would be a complete surprise to everyone but Barrow; his bosun had arranged to pick up the food when they passed Lands' End on their way back across the Channel. Davy had even chipped in for a bag of rare, imported oranges, one for each man. The December chill was working in their favor, as far as provisions were concerned—cold enough to keep the food from spoiling but warm enough that the oranges wouldn't freeze.

Davy... His presence on the *Mermaid* was both a joy and a continual source of anxiety for its captain. Marshall didn't know what would become of Davy when the Peace was broken. He didn't want to lose him from the crew, but—

"A moment, Captain?" The object of his musings appeared at his elbow.

"What is it, Mr. St. John?" He would be glad when they could dispense with this nonsense. The crew members who knew his real identity were trustworthy, and Sir Percy had said the St. John identity would be retired at the end of the year. That was fine with Marshall; he'd thought it a silly complication from the start.

"If you could come below, sir?" Davy asked blandly.

Marshall frowned. "Can it wait until the change of watch?"

His lover raised an eyebrow. "Captain Marshall, do you intend to rest at the end of this watch?"

He sighed. "Um..."

"My point precisely. Will, you can't avoid me indefinitely, this vessel's not big enough. I don't understand what it is that's bothering you. Was it something I said?"

"Of course not."

"What have I done, then?"

"Nothing!"

"All right." Davy's blue eyes were inscrutable as the sea. "There's nothing wrong, I've given no offense, but you haven't been coming into the cabin until long after I'm asleep, and you're up and gone before I wake. What am I to think?"

Marshall glanced around anxiously.

"There's no one in earshot, Will, you can trust me for that!"

He didn't know what to say. "I've had things on my mind..." Which was an understatement. All his resolution had deserted him after their escape; every time he had meant to approach Davy with a view to making love, he had been distracted by one thing or another, or one of the crew required his attention. Was he losing his nerve?

"Come below. Please?"

He sighed again. "Very well." He called to Barrow, gave him the helm, and followed Davy below to their shared cabin.

He was half-expecting to be pounced upon, was actually hoping for it; instead, Davy slipped the door-latch shut and faced him, his eyes troubled. "Will, what is wrong?"

"There's nothing wrong."

"I see." He ran a hand through his short, thick cap of hair. "No, I don't see. It's been over a month since you've shown any interest in what used to be a favorite activity; I thought there must be a reason. If I've done nothing, and nothing else is wrong..." He bit his lip, an old nervous habit that told Marshall the airy tone was a sham, and went on, "Shall I assume you've just lost interest? Should I—" He turned away, tugging at the line that held his cot suspended on his side of the tiny cabin they shared. "Would you prefer that I leave the *Mermaid* when we return to Portsmouth?"

The question struck Marshall like a blow. "What? No! Of course not!"

"Then, for God's sake, Will, *talk* to me!" His voice was low, but all the more intense for that. "I received news in the last mail-packet, when we turned the French delegation over to Sir Percy. Good news, I thought, but until I know your mind on this I'm no longer certain."

"What news?"

Davy shook his head. "Not until you tell me this: is it your wish that I stay with you when you return to regular duty in the Navy?"

He opened his mouth to say "Of course," and a hammer-blow of memory stopped him, the horror of seeing Davy carried belowdecks with a spreading red stain on his white waistcoat, the week of dread as they sailed back to Kingston, and the double loss—first when he thought

Davy had died, and then again after he'd healed, but duty took Marshall back to sea alone.

"How do you keep away the fear?"

Will had always been aware of his own mortality, but the constant expectation of his own death had allowed him to appear fearless. This, though, the razor-sharp knowledge that Davy might die, somehow that was even more frightening. Dying, especially a quick death, held little terror compared to the pain of going on alone.

Davy's question had no simple answer. And even though Marshall was captain of the *Mermaid*, that was one decision he had no right to make unilaterally. He hated the thought of having to choose. "Do you want to stay?"

In answer, Davy put a hand on either side of his face and pulled him into a kiss. Marshall was so cold from his long day on deck that his body was drawn to the warmth as much as anything. The closeness, the taste of Davy's mouth, woke a longing that he thought he had mastered, and he took his lover into his arms. A month! Had it really been that long?

When they stopped for breath, Davy said, "In case you didn't understand, that was 'yes.'" He extricated himself from the embrace, dropped into a careless slouch on the storage locker that served as a bench along the stern. It was a wanton slouch; it was a posture that said, *Come alongside, I'm prepared to be boarded.* "But only if I'm wanted."

Marshall sat beside him, telling himself that they had to sit close so they could speak without being overheard. "How can you doubt that?"

Davy wasn't giving an inch. "How can I not? You haven't touched me since we last discussed the matter. For all I know, you've taken it upon yourself to feel guilty that I was shot back in the Indies—"

The accusation was so dead-on that Marshall looked away.

"—and decided to punish yourself with a vow of celibacy."

"Davy, I—"

"And it never occurred to you," Davy continued, somewhat plaintively, "that you were also punishing *me.*" He grimaced comically, in contrast to his tone.

"Davy, I never intended any such thing! It's not— I only—" He ran out of protests and stopped to collect himself. Davy said nothing, merely waited. "I had not realized what a weight command would be. I am concerned about setting a good example for the crew. It seems difficult to find a time to be private." Even in his own ears, the excuses sounded hollow.

"Now you're prevaricating, Captain Marshall. Since we occupy the same cabin, opportunity seems to me to be the least of our difficulties." Davy took Will's hand, chafing life back into his half-numb fingers. "I have begun to wonder if I've somehow overstayed my welcome in your life. Étienne Beauchene…is a very attractive man. He wants you—I think he may even love you. And if I had died in Kingston, you'd be free."

Something wrenched in Will's chest. "No! Please, don't say such things." The very thought was like a knife in his heart. "Yes, Étienne is a good man…and if I did not love you, if I'd never known you, I might find him attractive. But— Davy, if you had died, I'd be as near dead myself as makes no difference. I lived for duty, from the time I left you in Jamaica. I think death would have been easier."

"And I can tell you from some experience that you're right. So tell me, please—" His fingers closed around Marshall's, holding tight. "Why do you push me away?"

"I want you safe!" Marshall blurted out, and immediately wished he hadn't.

"Oh, Will." Davy shook his head, smiling. "There is no safety outside the grave. At sea, at war... I could be shot, or run through, or blown up, or drowned."

"Exactly."

"But ashore, I could catch my death of cold, be run down by a horse, murdered by thieves, struck by lightning—"

"Oh, for heaven's sake!"

"No, honestly. I lost an uncle to a lightning strike. Kit's father was walking across his own lawn, and—"

"Damn it, I don't care if he was eaten by a tiger on London Bridge. Your chances of survival are better ashore."

"And so are yours! What would you have me do, Will, wall myself up in a monastery?" He leaned in for another kiss, a mere brushing of lips. "I don't think I could adapt to such a life. I would only corrupt the monks and be hanged for my pains."

Marshall was riven. Part of him was thrilled to know that his lover wanted to stay. Part of him wished that were not the case, and felt ashamed for wanting Davy at his side despite the danger. "Is there nothing I can say to make you reconsider?"

Davy shook his head. "No. Well, actually, yes. Look at me—" He touched Marshall's cheek, turned his face slightly so their eyes met. "*Look* at me, Will, and tell me you no longer care for me. If you can tell me that, and mean it, I'll remove myself as fast as ever I can." One corner of his mouth quirked up. "But I will know if you're lying."

It would only take a few words, and Davy would be safe. But with his eyes held by that merciless blue gaze, Will could not utter them. After a long, wordless moment, Will gave up. He pushed himself to his feet, pacing the three steps that were all the tiny cabin allowed. "I lost you twice in Kingston. I think once more would kill me."

"You have a risky job, Captain. That scraper you'll be wearing will make you a much better target than I. There's just as good a chance I could see you killed in action."

"Yes, but I—" Marshall turned, smiling ruefully at what he was about to say. "I wouldn't have to live through that. Ah, Davy... I never used to understand the notion of having a hostage to fortune. Now I do. And I hate it."

Davy looked up at him. "Is loneliness any better? Sooner or later, yes, one of us will die. It could be today, or next month, or fifty years from now, in peaceful sleep or the heat of battle. There's no way of knowing." He stood, blocking Marshall's restless wandering. "Would you forsake joy because there will someday be pain? Right now, at this moment, England is at peace and we are together. Why waste the time we have?"

He could not argue the sense of that, and Davy's face was so close... He bent his head; Davy flowed into his arms. After a time Marshall sighed and decided on a strategic retreat from a battle he could not possibly win. "You said that you had news. What is it?"

"Oh, that." With a smile, Davy patted his pocket. "Remember when we discussed the possibilities for my future career? I had in mind to become a ship's master under your command."

"It would be a waste of your training," Will said. "You'll be a lieutenant again, Davy, once the Peace breaks. Higher rank, with chance for advancement."

"True, but if I were to advance from that rank I'd be forced to take on a ship of my own, and we'd be apart until you became an Admiral. I've never seen the barky I'd take in trade for you. But look!" He produced a folded parchment with a flourish.

Though its seal had been broken, Marshall recognized it as an official document from the Admiralty. He sat on the bench to examine it more closely, recognizing what exactly it contained. "This certifies your qualification as a ship's master?"

Davy grinned, sitting close beside him. "Don't look so bottle-headed! Everyone knows what Boney's up to, and where's the harm in assuring there are qualified navigators to spare?"

"How did you manage this?" Will asked. "Without my knowing?"

"Kit, of course. It was no great trick for Baron Guilford to ask a favor and get his upstart cousin certified as a warrant officer. Particularly since Sir Percy and Captain Smith were ready to assure the Admiralty that I actually *was* qualified. Percy's only seconding what Sir Paul says, of course, but after what he and Mr. Drinkwater put me through before my Lieutenant's examination, I deserve it! Or should I say the three of you deserve it?"

"I think we all do." Navigational mathematics had not been Davy's strong suit, but between Marshall's tutoring, Drinkwater's patience, and Captain Smith's quizzes, he had finally learned what he needed to know. And Will had some fond memories of 'tutoring' Davy in the small hours, in quiet spots aboard the *Calypso*.

"So then, Captain Marshall, allow me to apply for the post of Ship's Master when you finally get your official command."

"That's 'if,' Mr. St. John," Marshall corrected.

"If and when, and I'll bet you a shilling it's before Midsummer Day."

"Done. I can always use the money."

They shook hands with mock-solemnity, and Davy let his breath out in a tremendous whoosh. "Will. On the subject of danger, sharing of, have we argued the case sufficiently to put it to rest, once and for all?"

It was a fair question, though Will knew that he would never cease worrying. "I think so. As long as fear for your safety does not affect my ability to command."

"Do you think it might?"

"I don't know, Davy. I simply do not know. I should hope not, but I cannot be sure. I think that it might. You mean more to me than any man aboard, or all the crew together." Or the ship itself, come to that. There was nothing in the world more important to Marshall than David Archer himself.

"We'll deal with it when we must, then," Davy said. "If, and when. If my presence does interfere with your command, I should have to go ashore. That would endanger the entire ship and crew. But knowing you, I don't believe it will. In the heat of battle, I could dance naked on the quarterdeck and you wouldn't notice."

"I believe we can forego that experiment, sir!"

"I believe we had better. I shouldn't want to risk losing any significant body parts." He rested a hand on Will's knee, and began to slide it slowly upward. "I would prefer to engage in other experiments, such as determin-

ing how long you can hold back after a month's absti-
nence."

"As long as you, I'll wager!"

"I shouldn't advise it." The hand found its target, and
Marshall found himself standing at attention while leaning back against the hull. "I've been keeping in practice,"
Davy murmured against his mouth, "and I'm quite certain
you have not!"

Marshall groaned as his body responded. "What? Not
now!"

"Why not?" He had the flap of Will's trousers unbuttoned and had somehow worked his fingers inside his
drawers.

"It's nearly time for the men's supper! Oh! God,
yes... Davy, wait, I—I need to take the helm while they
eat!"

"Will, you're the captain!"

"Yes, but—"

"The men won't be messing for half an hour."

"But—"

Davy got his left arm around Marshall's shoulders
while his free hand played merry hell with his captain's
composure. "Rank has its privileges!" he said, and put an
end to the conversation.

There was something extremely persuasive about the
way Davy kissed. No nonsense, no question of what he
had in mind, and no time wasted as he finished unbuttoning the underwear and freed Will's suddenly sensitive
cock. The feel of Davy's fingers closing tightly around it,
his thumb rubbing slowly over the tip, moistening it in the
cool air of the cabin, banished all other thought. Marshall
felt himself shivering in anticipation as Davy's tongue
carefully explored his mouth.

No matter how many times they did this, or under what circumstances, he was always a little in awe of his lover's enthusiasm. Not that he himself was reluctant, but in loveplay he often felt a bit embarrassed at his body's reactions and undignified behavior. What attraction Davy saw in a big-nosed, sharp-shinned scarecrow, he could not begin to imagine.

Davy, though—even with his golden hair cut so short it only brushed his collar, he had a beauty of grace and form that must surely win the love of anyone who saw him. His smile could melt a block of ice.

He was grinning now, the rascal, as he pulled back to assess the havoc he'd wrought. Continuing his slow, rhythmic caress of Marshall's cock, he asked, "Do you suppose you could spare a few minutes before you attend to the crew?"

With one arm pinned between them, Marshall had to satisfy himself with a grab for his lover's thigh. "You've raised the problem," he said, "you'd better deal with it."

Davy stood, slipping off his own shoes, and took hold of Marshall's waistband. "Lift your arse?"

When he did, Davy slid Will's trousers down around his knees, then loosened his own, and in a moment they were writhing together on the narrow bench, dignity thrown to the wind. It would've made more sense to balance on the cot, but that would have required getting up, and right now the only thing that mattered was the hot smooth length of Davy's cock sliding against his own, the pressure of his weight not quite enough, grabbing that beautiful arse with both hands and pulling Davy closer as they bucked together.

They had learned silence over the years; they could make love with no more noise than a bit of heavy breathing. But it *had* been a month, and Marshall found himself reaching the peak faster than he'd meant to, gasping in surprise when he felt his body spasm in release.

Davy bit his shoulder an instant later, then quieted. "Well," he said, taking some of his weight on his arms. "Lucky I didn't take that bet—though I do think you fired first!"

"It's not the same, alone," Marshall said. He ran a hand through Davy's hair. "Thank you for reminding me."

"My pleasure, Captain." Davy pulled his handkerchief from his jacket pocket and tidied them both. "May I invite you to a return engagement later this evening, after the crew has been fed and watered?"

He pulled himself back together swiftly, while Marshall was still luxuriating in the sense of well-being and fumbling with his drawers. "You may." He managed to balance with one hand against the hull while Davy helped tug his trousers back up. "In fact, I shall make amends to you for treating you so shabbily this past month. You must decide what you would like as your Christmas present. On Christmas night, after the men have had their treat, you will have yours."

That grin could be genuinely wicked. "With bells on?" Davy asked.

"I'm afraid not. Bells would be too noisy." That was safest, Will thought. It would not do to ask just what Davy thought the bells might be affixed to.

Chapter 12

The crew maintained a respectful silence while Captain Marshall read the Nativity from the Gospel of St. Luke. They enjoyed their feast down to the last mug of beer, exchanged small presents among themselves, then cleared the deck for dancing.

Despite the horrible noises Angus MacIvor scraped out of his fiddle, Marshall managed to enjoy the Christmas festivities. He found himself almost oblivious to the raucous screech, and even to the men capering on deck. He and Davy were sharing a bottle of wine. He'd given the men an extra ration of rum, which most of them preferred to wine anyway. The men were merry, though not drunk, but Marshall was still nursing his first glass, preoccupied with what Davy might ask of him once they'd retired to their cabin.

Davy seemed to sense his thoughtfulness. He joined in some of the Christmas carols, but every once in awhile he would shoot a quick look from those blue eyes, a look that sent fire down to the pit of Marshall's belly.

What was he going to ask?

Most of their trysts had been brief, limited to a few moments stolen from their duties, when they could find a bit of quiet and privacy, but every so often they'd had overnight shore leaves. They'd always gone through the precautionary sham of hiring a girl, then smuggling her out as fast as they could so they could spend the rest of the time exploring one another's bodies.

Dear God, they had been so young, back then. So young, so naïve... and so randy. The first time they had all night together, they had barely slept at all.

The last time...the last time they'd had days to spend together, they had both thought it would be the last time they'd ever see one another. They'd spent five blessed days at Lord Christopher St. John's estate in Jamaica, rediscovering each other and saying farewell. They had slept quite a lot then; Marshall had been exhausted by the weight of his first command, coupled with fear for his convalescent lover, and Davy had more enthusiasm than stamina. Every time they'd made love, it had seemed to wear him out, but that never stopped him for long. They'd done things that last night that they'd never done before or since. The night Will had been given command of the *Mermaid,* there had been so much to do that their reunion had been a poor imitation of what it should have been.

What would Davy ask? He liked it when they were both naked. So did Marshall, come to that, but he was always a little uneasy aboard ship, and he usually had at least his nightshirt on when they were together. Their cabin, like the *Mermaid* herself, was beautifully constructed but quite small, and the cots slung on either side made it difficult to brace oneself. Though Marshall had some theories he wanted to test, an interesting notion that would make good use of the physics of a suspended bed. The curves of curvature...

He cleared his throat as the thought of Davy's tempting arse swinging back and forth began to produce a trophy he didn't want to display on deck. As though hearing the thought, Davy looked up and grinned. "Penny for your thoughts, Captain?"

He narrowed his eyes. If Davy had learned to read minds, he should be hearing, *I'll get even with you for that one!* But in a way it gave him the chance to say a few words without having to make a speech, and the men would appreciate that, too.

"I was thinking," he said, noticing how the men quickly fell silent, "that in the ten years I've spent at sea," he nodded to Barrow and Klingler, who alone of the crew from the old *Titan* had known him as a green midshipman, "I've never seen a happier Christmas, a better crew, nor a finer ship." He raised his glass. "To your health, men, and a long, successful venture for us all!"

That brought a roar of approval, and three cheers for Captain Marshall, led by Barrow and joined enthusiastically by all the rest. MacIvor started sawing away again; Marshall recognized the first verse of the old song about a very dangerous female.

It was a cloudy morn when we set sail
and we were not far from the land
when our Captain he spied a fishy mermaid
with a comb and a glass in her hand

Marshall would have chosen a different tune. He didn't much like the story this song told—the unnamed ship in the tale wound up sinking to the bottom of the sea.

Davy rose and wandered over to lean against the railing where Marshall stood. "Pay attention," he said under his breath. "They've rewritten it for you."

Marshall set his teeth against the screeching violin and managed what he hoped looked like a smile.

And the ocean waves do roll
and the stormy winds do blow
and we brave tars go skippin' on the deck

while the landlubbers lie down below, below
While the landlubbers lie down below!

Then up spoke the Captain of our gallant ship
and a brave young skipper was he
"Well, no fishy mermaid will ever frighten us
For this crew is the bravest on the sea!"

Another chorus, God help us, Will thought. It wasn't that he didn't like music. He liked it very well indeed—but between MacIvor's ill-tuned fiddle and a foretopman who couldn't carry a tune if his life depended on it, Will wasn't sure this performance could even be considered music.

Then up spoke the owner of our gallant ship
and a brave young tradin' man was he
"No mermaid will scare us, we've got a job to do
A fishy lass will never frighten me!"

Marshall leaned close to his friend. "Seems you've been included as well," he said as the crew ground through another chorus.

Then up spoke the bosun of our gallant ship
and a wise old sailin' man was he
"Our Mermaid's a good lass, she'll bring us home again
She'll keep us safe upon this stormy sea!"

Finally, the end was in sight, and the crew finished up the final chorus with more enthusiasm than skill. When the last landlubber was lyin' down below, Davy inclined his head subtly. Finished, at last! Marshall nodded his approval.

"No landlubbers on *this* ship!" Barrow said emphatically.

"And no nonsense about going to the bottom of the

sea!" Marshall responded. "Thank you, men! Mr. St. John and I are going to retire to our dinner, and leave you to your celebration. Merry Christmas!"

"A fine speech, Captain." Davy said as he followed Marshall into their cabin and slid the folding table from its brackets behind his cot. "Brief and to the point. Would you care for a little more wine?"

"Not just yet." One folding chair fit on either side of the table, and he lit the candle lantern that hung above it. They'd barely finished setting up when the steward arrived with their dinner, a nicely stewed chicken, with potatoes and carrots and bread bought when they'd been in port two days before. And coffee, for which Marshall had developed an irrational fondness as the Beauchenes' guest.

"Well?" he demanded, as they enjoyed their meal. "Have you determined what you would like for Christmas?"

"I'm still thinking," Davy said. And he said little more until they were finishing the juicy slices of their own oranges. The sweet tartness on Marshall's tongue reminded him somehow of Davy, and he asked once again.

"I'll tell you when Clement has cleared the dishes," Davy promised. "But in the meantime, this is for you." And he held out a small package, neatly wrapped in brown paper and held shut with a bit of red ribbon. It proved to be a pair of gloves of soft black leather, exquisitely tailored and lined with lambswool.

"Oh... These are too grand, Davy!"

"Try them on."

They fit perfectly, of course, and he could remember one morning sometime back when Davy had made a point of comparing their hands, Will's fingers much longer than his own neatly shaped ones.

"They'll never fit anyone else properly, so you must keep them." Davy leaned forward, eyes twinkling. "I can't tell you how distressing it is to have your icy digits inserted into places where they can get warm," he whispered.

Their steward, Clement, chose that moment to return and clear the table. Marshall took the opportunity to retrieve the present he had bought for Davy before they had first sailed out in the *Mermaid,* a small collection of poetry that he had taken pains to determine his friend did not possess.

"It's beautiful, Will," Davy said, opening the leather covers reverently. "Some old friends... and some of these I've never read!"

"I'll never have your gift for words," Marshall said, embarrassed. "I'd write the stuff for you myself, if I could."

He was rewarded with a look of such uncomplicated affection that he took Davy's hand, across the table. "Will you tell me, now, what you would like?"

"Whatever you wish to give," Davy said.

"What?"

"Will, I've known you for seven years now," he said, mischievousness replacing the softer sentiment. "And one thing I have learned: when given an objective and free use of your imagination, you always excel. So...I would like to be ravished, by whatever means you choose."

Marshall felt as he had one Christmas when he was six years old, and a kindly woman, one of his father's parishioners, had given him a whole sack of biscuits. One sort had nuts, another raisins, another was dusted in sugar... it had taken him most of an hour to decide which to eat first.

"I'm going to stretch my legs," Davy said, still smiling. "I'll be back momentarily." He didn't bother to put his greatcoat on, which seemed to indicate a short trip.

Clement came in as he left, to put away the table, but Marshall told him to leave it up. "Mr. St. John and I are going to have a game of cribbage before we turn in," he said. "We may stay up late, and we'll attend to the furniture. You're off-duty for the night, and a merry Christmas to you!"

He passed a half-crown to the grateful steward. It was very, very pleasant to have a little money to spare for generosity, and having observed Captain Smith's treatment of his cabin servants, back aboard the *Calypso,* he was sure the investment was worthwhile.

He put the table away immediately; they were going to play, but not cribbage! A towel stuffed into the deckglass assured them a bit of privacy—barring the outbreak of war, of course, but it was unlikely that the French would attack on Christmas night.

A tap at the door, and Davy poked his head inside. "Ready or—wha—?!" He stifled a yelp as Marshall caught his wrist, yanking him all the way into the room.

"One ravishment," Marshall whispered, "as ordered." He pulled Davy against him, capturing his mouth in a fierce kiss. But Davy was seldom at a loss for long, and as Marshall lifted him in his arms, Davy wrapped his legs around Marshall's hips. Overbalanced, he tipped forward, pinning his lover against the bulkhead.

"Mister St. John!" he gasped. "If you please!"

"Mm?"

"Who's ravishing whom, here?"

Davy blinked, his eyes slightly unfocused. "Oh." He

unwound himself, grinding against Marshall as he lowered himself to his feet. "Was I giving offense?"

"Not at all! I only expected—if you wish to be ravished, sir, you might be a little more receptive!"

"Receptive? I thought I was!" Davy grinned. "Very well, then—what shall I do?"

"Allow me to demonstrate." Marshall reached up and began to unbutton his lover's short jacket. David St. John, civilian, dressed a trifle more elegantly than his naval predecessor, but for ordinary shipboard life a grey wool jacket and darker trousers served well enough.

As the buttons yielded beneath his fingers, Marshall was aware of Davy's eyes upon him; he felt his face growing warm, and reminded himself that *he* was doing the seduction here.

Silly notion. As he finished with the jacket and started undoing the silky blue waistcoat, Davy sighed, and Will felt his hands tremble. It was silly; they'd been rolling around only a couple of hours before, and here he was, eager as a bridegroom.

He slid the jacket and waistcoat together from Davy's shoulders, leaning forward for another kiss. He felt Davy's hands on his hips, and they leaned against each other gently this time, rocking back and forth with the motion of the sea.

I could stay like this forever, Marshall thought foolishly.

But this wasn't ravishing; this was romantic mooning. "Mr. St. John," he murmured, "would you object if I remove the rest of your clothing?"

"I would be crushed if you did not."

It was chilly in the cabin, and damp, but not quite chilly enough to see one's breath, and he intended to keep

Davy sufficiently warm even without his clothing. Nuzzling down the side of his neck, Marshall moved around behind his lover, pulling Davy close to his body's warmth and alternating nips and kisses while he worked loose Davy's trouser buttons. As the clothing fell to his ankles Davy pressed backward. "God, Will—"

"Patience, sir. I intend to make a proper job of this!" He let his hands roam over the front of Davy's body. The scar of his terrible wound was smaller now, but he felt a pang as his fingers brushed across it. They had come so close, so very close... "Davy..."

"You mustn't say—"

"I know. But this is important. I love you, Davy." It was difficult to say the words. Why? Why should the greatest truth of his life be so hard to express? An awkward truth, even a dangerous one, but all the more precious for that. "I love you."

Davy's head fell back against Marshall's shoulder, and he twisted around for another kiss. He was all smooth warm skin and supple strength, turning like an eel within the embrace. Marshall scooped him up and deposited him in one of the cots, then pulled off boots and stockings, leaving that beautiful body naked against the striped ticking.

He *was* beautiful, the loveliest thing Marshall had ever seen. Even with the golden mane shorn short, the sight of that strong curve of shoulder, the scattering of wiry hair across the broad chest, smooth flat belly...

Marshall had never had any artistic pretensions. He could appreciate the sun's bright rays angled low over water, or white sails straining against the wind; paintings and statuary had never moved him. But this living, breathing work of art was something else altogether. When he looked at Davy's naked form, the very sight awoke the memory of how wonderful that body felt against his own.

He took a moment to be sure the door was latched shut and shed his own clothing as he returned to the cot. He barely noticed the cabin's temperature; he felt very warm indeed. "Now, then, this matter of ravishment..."

Davy merely smiled, and held out a hand. Marshall took it, caressed it, and brought it to his lips. Davy had done this for him, once, and it had nearly driven him out of his mind. He licked the palm of that small strong hand, flicking his tongue between the fingers, then ran his tongue from wrist to elbow in quick short strokes. As he neared the armpit he was overwhelmed by the scent of this beautiful man, his beautiful lover. Davy was habitually clean, but sex had its own scent, and their earlier encounter had marked him. Marshall's cock hardened as that most particular musk worked its magic on his brain and body.

He met Davy's eyes. The glass of wine Will had earlier could not account for the flush that heated his lips as he slid them down that warm shoulder. The blue eyes slid shut as his lips fastened on a nipple; Davy's chin tilted up as he gasped and shivered. Marshall felt a bit unsteady himself, and held tight to the cot as he ran his tongue across the sensitive nub. He let his other hand caress his lover's tight belly, roving down to the springy curls that surrounded the now rampant cock.

Davy squirmed and whimpered under the dual teasing. The tip of his cock was wet already, and Marshall worked the fluid around with his thumb and transferred his attentions to the other nipple. "Are you feeling ravished yet?" he mumbled around the tiny nub, and gave it another careful pinch."

"You're getting there," Davy said breathlessly. His nails dragged across Marshall's shoulder. "In fact, I— oh!"

Marshall had taken a firm grasp of the main objective, and began licking a slow trail from chest to groin. He paused to kiss and lick the navel. His own wasn't especially sensitive, but such attentions drove Davy mad. When his whimper indicated that objective was achieved, Will proceeded to mount his main assault.

Such a silly thing, a cock. The Great Architect must have a truly bizarre sense of humor. But when attached to a beloved, what a perfect gauge of passion.

He had not paid such homage often. In the years since they'd become lovers, Davy had often thrown dignity to the wind and worshipped Will's body with his mouth. Marshall, squeamish, had offered but had usually been relieved when the offer was declined.

Now, for reasons he did not understand himself, Davy's cock became an object of veneration. He slid the foreskin down, rubbing the slippery head against his lips, delighting in the stifled cry the movement produced. Holding it tight, he ran his tongue delicately around its head. Davy's fingers tangled in his hair, and a whispered, "Oh, yes!" delighted him. And then he took it wholly into his mouth, letting his tongue move against its length, and Davy let out a low moan and rose up to meet him.

He feasted. Why this had bothered him before he could not say, but some inner censor had at last been silenced, and he took such delight in pleasing this precious human being that he felt he had almost become some other person. There was no room here for William Marshall's sense of dignity, the burden of rank or position. There was only Will, who loved Davy, who was whimpering, "Yes, please!" and writhing on the cot in complete abandon.

He cupped Davy's balls in one hand, reaching back to tickle his sensitive opening, and Davy trembled, thrust and cried out quietly as he pushed Will's face against him and arched, tensing as his body spent itself, and then relaxing completely.

Marshall snatched the bottle of wine from the table and took a long swallow, then draped himself over his lover and pulled the blanket over them both. So strange; he had not reached his own satisfaction, but Davy's pleasure was one he could feel in a magical, nearly physical way; he shared somehow in that release. He was conscious of Davy's arms going around him before he dozed.

It could have been minutes that he lolled in the pleasant warmth of his lover's embrace; it might have been longer. He wasn't sure he ever really fell asleep. But eventually the gentle rocking of the sea brought him back to the awareness that he had not completed his task, and that however satisfied Davy might be, his own body was ready to be rewarded for its restraint.

He raised his eyelids a fraction, and saw Davy's blue eyes an inch away. "Are your prepared for further debauchery?" he asked courteously.

"Ye gods, Captain, I'd nearly forgotten what a determined fellow you can be." Davy tangled both hands in Marshall's hair and pulled him close for a long, involved kiss. "I shall await further debauching at your earliest convenience."

Davy was such fun in bed. There was no other way to put it; his capacity for enjoyment was amazing. Marshall never ceased to marvel at how a man who had survived so much pain could feel and share such joy. Whatever the cause, he was blessed to have such a lover.

"Well, then." He assessed the situation, realizing that there wasn't room for really inspired ravishing. "I propose to leave no inch of you untouched." He suited his action to the words, holding Davy close with one arm slid beneath his head while the other was left free to roam.

Davy's lips parted, an obvious invitation for another kiss, as Marshall's fingers slipped into the crevice of his arse. They didn't have much room to move, but Davy crooked one leg up over Marshall's hip, giving him free access. For a little while he lost himself in the taste and feel of his lover, the heat as his searching fingers found their goal. Davy jerked forward with a yip of surprise as he slid one finger inside. "That's *cold!"*

"My apologies, sir. But you may be chillier still." Shifting suddenly, he regained his feet beside the cot, turning Davy as he moved so the smaller man was now lying crosswise upon it, his arse caught on the edge and his legs hanging over the side. "Wait a moment." He grabbed the pillow and wedged it beneath Davy's head at the far side of the cot, then surveyed his prize. "Are you comfortable?"

Davy seemed to consider his position, Marshall standing between his outstretched legs with one knee crooked over each elbow. If Marshall let go, he'd slide right onto the floor, but he'd know Will would not let that happen. He stretched his arms out to either side, along the starboard edge of the cot, grinning in a most abandoned fashion. "Quite comfortable, thank you. And yourself?"

Marshall took a step closer, bracing Davy's rump against his own belly. "Doing very nicely." He surveyed the riches spread out before him, and could not resist stroking the strong thighs spread so invitingly. He felt

Davy quiver as he dragged his fingernails slowly across the tender flesh. "I hardly know where to begin."

Davy was watching him, his gaze so intense it felt like a touch. His eyes closed, though, when Will's fingers reached his nipples. Those soft pink lips parted soundlessly as he gasped for air. "Willll…"

"What would you like?" Marshall asked. "Tell me, Davy…"

He leaned forward, caught the sweet lips with his own, tasting, probing. He could feel Davy hardening against him once more, and his own body responded a hundredfold.

"What do you want?"

Davy's body lifted up against his; there was a sharp twinge as their cocks brushed together. "—me.." Davy murmured.

"What's that?"

"Fuck me! Damn it, Will! It's been so long—"

He tried to catch Marshall's arse, but his arms weren't long enough. Will laughed softly. "You want to be thoroughly ravished, then?"

"*Yes!*"

And his own body was saying *now!* Quickly, he found the jar of salve in the canvas bag slung from the hook that supported the hammock. He leaned down to kiss Davy again as he took the cork out of the jar, scooped out a fingerful of the salve, and covered his own cock with the stuff. He slid what was left into Davy, and smiled as his lover bore down around his invading fingers. "Patience, Mr. St. John!"

"To hell with patience, Will, *take me!*"

The heated whisper was like oil on fire, but Marshall had sworn to himself, long ago, that he would never, under any circumstances, risk causing Davy pain. So he took his time, easing his fingers in, using a long deep kiss as distraction while he made sure his lover was ready to receive him.

When he finally positioned himself and slid inside, he was near to bursting, and the tight slick heat of Davy closing around him drove him mad with passion. He slid all the way in, and Davy squeezed, and he threw himself against his lover, letting the cot swing wildly. "Buggery boxes," he'd heard these cots called, and justly so. They put things at a perfect level.

He didn't know how long he stood there, leaning into Davy, letting the swing of the cot do most of the work. Their earlier tryst made a difference; it had reduced the urgency, given him time to enjoy this sweet friction as their bodies danced together. He looked down, met Davy's eyes, and it felt as though their very souls were joined as deeply as their bodies. "I love you, Davy. Love you, love you..." How very strange, to have his thoughts so free while their bodies were slamming together like two parts of a pile-driver. "Love you..."

"Will..." Davy was flushed, lips reddened, sweat beading his beautiful face. He caught Marshall's wrists. "Harder, Will. Please...."

But he couldn't manage harder. The cot was a delightful platform, but even leaning forward he couldn't use his whole weight.

"The floor, damn it!" Davy gasped. "Put me on the floor!" Halfway up, his nails dug into Marshall's arse. "Harder. *Please!*"

The temptation was irresistible. Marshall snatched at the mattress from his own cot, yanked it onto the floor, and dragged both Davy and the other mattress out of the other cot. He was barely able to break the fall as he bore his lover down to the deck, stifling his own cry as they both made contact and the impact drove him deeper in. Davy's legs wrapped around the small of his back and they rocked together like mad things, his own breath coming in short gasps as Davy's teeth closed on his shoulder, a sharp pinch that sent a jolt through to his cock—

"Love you love you love you love you…" He was sobbing, wheezing, and then riveted in a shattering climax that seemed to set off Davy's own. He felt the warm spurt against his belly as he cried out against Davy's neck.

It took a little while to get his senses back. He rolled to his side, cuddling his lover close. A sense of warmth and happiness seeped through him, like hot soup or strong drink, and better than either. He was naked, gloriously naked, without rank or dignity or fear, and at least for the moment he knew what was truly important. "I love you," he said once more, brushing the hair out of Davy's beautiful blue eyes. "Davy, I love you."

"Yes," Davy said, eyes shining. "So long as we both shall live."

The phrase was familiar and right, though he had never expected to hear it regarding himself and anyone else, much less another man. But Davy voiced what was in both their hearts. "Yes," he agreed. "For better or worse."

Davy laughed ruefully. "I think we've seen both, now. Kiss me?"

He did. But it was December, and it was cold. Before long they were cuddling for warmth more than anything, and Will reached up to snag a blanket. "We'd best go to bed," he said, regretfully.

"Pull down all the blankets," Davy advised. "We're

fine as we are."

He did; it was going to take all the blankets to keep off the chill. "But the men—"

"I spoke to Barrow," Davy said. "We have until morning, Will. It isn't much of a Christmas present...but we can sleep together tonight, if you like. All night long, together."

The joy was sharp as a knife; he could not stop the tears. Davy held him tight, and kissed him, and pulled the blanket close. "Merry Christmas, love."

~The End~

About the Author

Lee Rowan has been writing since childhood, but professionally only since spring of 2006, with the publication of her Eppie-winning novel, *Ransom*. She is a lady of a certain age, old enough to know better but young enough to do it anyway. A confirmed bookaholic with a wife of many years, she is kept in line by a cadre of cats and a dog who gets her away from the computer and out of the house at least once a day.

You can visit her on the Web at www.lee-rowan.net

Coming soon from
Cheyenne Publishing

Book Four of the Royal Navy Series:

Home is the Sailor

by Lee Rowan

LaVergne, TN USA
17 March 2011
220549LV00001B/245/P